The One-Legged Cowboy

John Herold

Lime Press

The One-Legged Cowboy by John Herold

ISBN: 978-1-953584-16-8 (Paperback)
ISBN: 978-1-953584-15-1 (eBook)

Printed in the United States of America.

Lime Press LLC
425 West Washington Street
Suffolk VA, 23434 Suite 4
https://www.lime-press.com/

Foreword

The cowboys' life was not glamorous. It was hard work every day and into the evenings as well. The cowboy was paid one to four dollars a month to herd the unruly and skittish longhorn cattle, to rope the strays and brand them, and to be able to drive the herds many, many miles to the railroads in Kansas for shipment back East. The cowboy knew he could be crushed under a stampede or even be hit by lightning on the open plains. He was fortunate if he made it to a town once or twice a year.

It didn't take a degree from a college, but a lot of guts and doggedness to be a real cowboy. The cowboy was usually a young man with little ties to home and a strong desire to roam. He was extremely devoted to his partners on the range and would die fighting for them.

He wore the same clothes every day and ate whatever the chuck wagon cook gave him. He carried a bedroll tied behind the saddle and slept on the ground regardless of the weather. He became as hard as nails but had graciousness to all whom he met. He was a real hero of the Old West.

Table of Contents

Chapter

1

The clouds have no water, neither does Joe.

Thunder's hooves were kicking up billowy clouds of dust as Joe Lundy kept forcing his horse up the steep wall of a dry arroyo. It had not rained for several days, and halfway up the ascent, Thunder's legs slipped on some loose stones, which caused the horse's spine to flex hard, creating great pain. The horse started kicking and shaking its hindquarters, while still attempting to climb higher. For a brief second, Joe thought he was riding one of the bucking broncos back at the ranch. He shook the reins and dug his spurs deeper into Thunder's sides, but it had little affect. Something was wrong, and Joe knew it. Thunder had never acted this way in the eight years that he had owned him. The experience was baffling, and Joe knew he had little time to react.

Just as Joe saw the top of the wall, he caught a glimpse of Thunder's right rear leg slipping into a badger hole. The beautiful black stallion panicked and reared, kicking its front legs very high into the azure sky. It was too much. Both horse and rider flipped over backward and slid down the wall.

Horse and rider lay at the bottom, both badly hurt. A broken leg would seal Thunder's fate. A shaken and dazed Joe, all six feet of him, struggled to get to his feet. He wobbled; his mind was in a state of confusion as he tried to get his bearings. Pulling a bandana off his neck, he started wiping the dirt and dust off his face as he watched Thunder's futile attempts to get up. Thunder kept shaking his head, his black mane rippling in the air, his right rear leg folded beneath him.

Many years of riding on the open plain had taught Joe what he must do. With a badly sprained right hand and a damaged right leg, both hurting like hell, he moved closer to the saddle. With his left hand, he, awkwardly, pulled his rifle out of the scabbard. Joe took aim as best as he could and fired just once. As he dropped to his knees, the sorrow that came upon him was so intense that it briefly masked any of his physical pain. Thunder's head flopped down hard on the dirt, causing a plume of dust; his mane becoming just a flat black ribbon covering Joe's crushed canteen.

"Goodbye, partner. I'll miss you." They were all the words Joe could muster.

A short time later, hobbling on his one good leg and trying to balance a saddle on his shoulder, Joe Lundy found himself attempting to cross Utah's rugged Wastatch Basin. For many years, he had heard rumors that no white man had ever been able to do it, but he was alone, and he knew he had little choice: either try to make it back to the ranch or die.

Walking in the sweltering heat, Joe was becoming well aware that the blazing sun was sucking the water out of his body at a rapid rate and causing him to lose his strength and stamina. He had no source of water and now was convinced his only reason for staying alive was his dogged determination. He thought if the Indians could travel across the basin, why couldn't he? He pushed onward.

As the sun traveled across the sky, Joe began to sway, missing a step. The air was completely still. The sun's rays were baking his body like a damn potato in a campfire. Time was losing its meaning. Joe was only aware of two things: the intermittent beads of sweat hanging from his eyelashes and that innate fortitude he had to stay alive. He would stumble, but he knew he had to keep moving forward.

As the day dragged on, Joe started to realize he was in a different part of the basin. The change was not easy. His steps were intermittent as his boots twisted in the rough sand. At one point, Joe lost his balance and fell facedown. The saddle had a handcrafted high arch shape to it, and it had fallen over Joe's head, creating a small air pocket. It offered a bit of shade, but the small pebbles in the hot sand soon pitted his face with burnt marks. He reasoned this is what a steer must feel like at branding time.

With his one good hand, Joe reached under the saddle and scraped out a deeper groove for extra space. Now, the deeper sand felt much cooler. He had some relief but wasn't satisfied. Joe decided to turn his head upright, resting his chin on the sand. Having a better view, Joe could see in the distance a haze floating just above the land, and what lied ahead. It did look hopeful, lifting his spirits some. He had renewed vigor. He rested a little while longer, and then pushed the saddle aside. Joe had to wrestle with himself to stand erect. Once stable, he picked up the saddle and continued onward.

Joe spotted the outline of a small mesa with a few trees beyond the haze. Could it be the real thing or was it a mirage? He wondered. He prayed hard it wasn't a mirage, and that water might be there. He estimated the mesa was a mile away. He thought he heard a sound and looked back. He saw two coyotes following him. They had noticed his shirt was hanging loose and flesh like. It had turned from a tan to a mottled brown from all his sweat and dust, and it was sagging over his leather belt. Strangely, his forehead now felt bone dry. He knew the mesa was his only chance to avoid a heat stroke or death. He had to reach the top of it before nightfall. He labored on.

It became late afternoon. The sun's rays had passed their zenith. The hungry coyotes watched as Joe barely made it to the top of the mesa. He was hunched over, gasping for all the air he could get. Between those gasps he caught sight of two old cottonwood trees not more than twenty yards away. He was sure those trees meant water was close by. Joe could feel his chest pressing hard on the barrel end of his rifle. He didn't care. He was a gambler. To him, the cards were dealt. He knew he would have to use all his remaining strength to reach those damn trees.

Tottering from side to side, Joe placed one boot forward, then the other. He fought hard to stay upright. To bolster his fortitude, he, even, started mumbling profanities to himself, but he could not ignore the severe pain that had increased in his right leg. A few drops of blood kept oozing out from beneath the chap. His right hand had been so badly sprained, that he could barely hold on to anything. He knew he was facing total exhaustion and death. He even began to imagine seeing his skeleton lying among the many bleached buffalo bones that used to dot the basin.

Taking those last laborious steps proved to be the hardest. When his left hand was about to touch one of the trees, he let go of the rifle. The hair trigger hit a tree root poking up out of ground. He heard a click, but nothing happened. He lost his grip on the saddle too, and it hit the ground with a thud. He scanned the area looking for any signs of water. There were none, just a dried up gully.

"You son-of-a-bitch" Joe could barely get the words out. He knew cottonwood trees usually grew near a spring or a stream. Why did these damn trees offer him no water? Joe knew he was one tough hombre, and the cowboy life was all he ever wanted, but he realized he was losing the battle to stay alive.

Leaning against the tree trunk, Joe tried hard to stand tall, but couldn't. He removed his weathered Stetson hat, and let it fall. He took the end of the bandana that was draped around his neck, and attempted to wipe his dusty brow. When he tried to swallow, he discovered his throat had constricted. He thought of the empty canteen that was under Thunder's body, and envisioned having a shot of Crazy Dave's Saloon whiskey. He also knew a sip of cool water would do quite nicely.

Joe squinted again at the horizon. He saw nothing but that haze still hanging over the land. He sagged. The late afternoon heat had been so unrelenting, and the air so still that he couldn't understand how any Indian could ever survive the rigors of living in this arid, hostile land, especially doing it on bare feet.

Joe tried to find some relief. His gasping for air was beginning to ease up, so he decided to rub his eyes again for better vision. He could see the sun was setting behind the tallest peaks of the Uinta mountain range. That sight seemed to give him a new sense of comfort. The ranch he lived on was somewhere out there. In his dazed mind, the reality of yesterday began to speak to him.

It had been a very tough day, driving mostly longhorn cattle off the open range, and back to the ranch. They were like wild animals used to their freedom, and would not obey the sound of his whip. Some of the ornery ones would constantly stray from the main herd. Being an excellent scout in the Indian wars, Joe could find any trail, and he soon discovered the tracks of two large bulls that had wondered off.

Without alerting anybody, Joe Lundy quickly deviated from the other cowhands and had ridden miles before he caught sight of them. They were in a deep, dry arroyo near a damp spot, licking the tops of wet mud. Nearby, a few buffaloes were wallowing in a dust bowl they had made. Having seen this problem before, Joe knew all he had to do was to ride down one of the steep walls, circle get around behind the bulls, and crack his whip over their heads. The sounds would vibrate inside their horns, and spook them back to the main herd while the buffaloes would panic in fear, and scatter in all directions. He knew the owner of the Delta D ranch would be quite pleased. They were his two of his prized bulls, and worth a fortune in stud fees. Joe always got extra compensation for bringing the most difficult ones home.

The last of Joe's energy finally gave out, and he dropped to the ground. He was able to rest his back against the saddle. Sleep overcame him so quickly he did not have time to unwrap his bedroll. However, a devilish thought did cross his mind. Perhaps, drinking and playing cards with the other cowhands around a campfire late last night might have had something to do with his present condition. He probably drank too much. He also knew he was better at card playing than most of the cattle drivers, and remembered, in particular, two card players, Zack and Jonas, who seemed quite upset when he won the big pot. Zach was the smaller of the two, who liked to pick his teeth with his shiny, pointed skinning knife while staring at you with his cold beady eyes. But now it didn't matter. Pain or no pain, Joe's mind shut down. His eyelids closed. He was out cold.

Chapter
2

A rustle in the leaves of the old cottonwoods signaled a wind from the north was approaching fast. Sometimes, the summer winds developed into a whirligig, or miniature tornado. Lying as close to the ground as you could, preferably in a gully, and holding onto something solid while praying were the recommended rules of safety.

The wind intensified rapidly. The branches of the cottonwoods swayed erratically to the wind's tempo. A loud crack occurred. One large branch splintered, and came falling down, just missing Joe's head. Fast asleep, he flinched just a little.

A silent figure dropped down from another branch, and without hesitation, kicked the saddle aside, and stretched out beside Joe's body. The figure grabbed the fallen tree branch in one hand, Joe's hair in the other, and held on for dear life.

A tremendous amount of debris: twigs, grasses, dirt, stones, collected above them, and then fell upon them as the rotating winds suddenly died as suddenly as they started. In a matter of seconds, the moon was starting to make its appearance, and all was quiet once again.

As Joe awakened, the glare of the morning sun came into his eyes. He squinted hard to make sense of his surroundings. A neat pile of leaf litter, and other debris lay beside him. He realized his lips were moist, and he did not feel so thirsty. He touched his face and it felt oily. When he did try to move his right leg, however, he felt the intense pain all over again.

Then, Joe caught the whiff of something baking.

As he turned his head away from the sun, Joe could see a young Indian brave, perhaps fourteen years old, kneeling over a small fire, stirring something in a pot. The smoke from the fire was rising in little puffs, and heading toward the sky.

The Indian brave looked at Joe. At first, he showed no emotion.

Red lines of paint marked his cheeks. A single hawk feather was stuck in his black hair.

Joe attempted to move once again, but the pain in his leg was just too great, so he raised his sore right hand indicating a sign of peace. What did this young brave want? Joe thought. His saddle? His rifle? His clothing? His life?

A smirk appeared on the brave's face. "I know the peace signal.

Everyone does. It is like somebody saying "Ahoy" at sea."

Joe was surprised. In this part of the country, no Indian schools existed. "You speak good English. Where did you learn it?"

"You ask me. I tell you." Joe could see a fierce look had developed. "When I was six years old, men in blue uniforms took me away from my parents, and sent me to a boarding school in the East. I was there for seven years until I decided to run away, and come back to my parents and my tribe."

The brave removed the pot from the fire, and placed it on a large flat rock.

Joe decided to change the subject. He could see the pot was old and dented. "Where did you get the pot?"

"I found it next to the ruts in the ground made by wagon wheels.

Some settlers passing through must have dropped it, I guess."

Joe touched his thin pencil moustache, and then ran his fingers through his thinning hair. His scalp was sore. "My hair feels like someone tried to yank it out."

There was no response.

Joe looked around, his eyes searching for something.

"What happened to my hat?"

The Indian brave pulled it out of some debris lying next to a tree, and handed it to him. Joe grabbed it with his left hand, and after some maneuvering, placed it on his head exactly the way he liked it.

The sudden glare off the front of Joe's hat caught the boy's attention. "What is that round thing on the band of your hat?"

"It's a gold locket."

"What's it for?" asked the boy.

"It's personnel," Joe said abruptly.

Joe thought for a moment. He felt he needed to know more about this brave who had saved his life, but he had to be careful. "Did you ever find your parents?"

"Yes, but they were dead." "Dead?"

"They were so sad at losing their freedom to hunt buffalo on this land, and losing me, that one winter day they sat outside in the cold and froze to death."

Joe could sense the Indian boy was really hurt by the loss, but more willing to talk.

"So may I ask why are you here?"

"My uncle, Lone White Feather, said it was my time. I must go out on this land alone, and find my future. I must carry on the legacy of my father. I was to eat little. I was to wait many days for the spirits to speak to me, and give me guidance and courage. Only then, could I return to my tribe."

"What tribe is that?"

The Indian brave stared into the pot. "Nuchu. You know us as the mountain Utes. The boy was a little annoyed.

"You ask too many questions."

"Sorry. Please continue talking."

"I walked many miles, and slept under the stars, afraid. The wolves howled, and the coyotes followed me all the time waiting for me to die. I became lost. Everything looked the same. Then I found these trees. I climbed to the top of one of them, and waited. Here the Great Spirit spoke to me in a dream. He said I must wait for one who needs you. Follow him."

Now Joe looked a bit annoyed. "So you were already in one of the trees when I came by. And now, you expect me to be your leader?"

"I know my right leg and right hand will always be useless. I have seen other cowhands suffer the same fate. His horse steps into a damn prairie dog hole, or a badger hole. The horse breaks its leg, and stumbles, throwing the rider forward, or in my case, backward. If the cowhand is alive, he shoots the horse, and hopes he can make it back to the ranch house. I am a crippled cowpoke. My riding and roping days are over. This is all that I am, and ever will be. I can't lead anybody."

The Indian's voice held firm. "The Great Spirit has spoken. I will dress your wounds, and make a splint for you to stand up, and travel. I have sent several smoke signals before you woke up. Someone will find us soon."

Joe knew he had lost the argument. "By the way, what is your name?"

"Gray Owl Waiting. But you can call me Gray."

"I have never seen a Gray Owl around these parts."

"They live north of here in the great forest, and I must find one soon. It was my mother's last wish. I was told she believed it had magical powers."

"Magical powers? Isn't that feather in your hair good enough?" a confused Joe asked.

"It is a hawk feather my uncle gave me, but I must find my own."

"What's that notch in the top of the feather mean?"

"That notch as you call it shows the first time my uncle had a coup."

Joe smiled a little. "Yeah, I know what a coup is. It is touching the enemy with a stick to prove how brave you are."

Gray was surprised. "Yes, that is right."

"I was an Indian scout once."

Gray thought for a moment. He knew he needed Joe's help." There is a girl named White Flower, in my tribe, who I want to marry, but I have no horses to give her parents. A gray eagle feather would be enough to convince her parents I love her. I need to find one."

"Okay, Gray. You go do what you have to. You go north, but leave me out of it. I cotton to no one, and my name, by the way, is Josiah Lundy. But you can call me Joe."

Joe noticed a green thing attached to Gray's rawhide belt. "What's that in your belt? A good luck charm of some kind?"

Gray, a little nervous, touched his belt.

"You mean this?" "Yeah."

"It is a piece of what white man calls a Beavertail plant. My uncle made me carry it. I use the oily stuff inside it. It's like aloe. I put it on all the burnt marks on your face and hands."

"So that's why my face feels so oily."

Gray poked the contents in the pot with a piece of dried weed, and then pulled it out. The weed was clean.

"No more talking. Let's eat. I made Indian bread from the little bit of flour I had left. It's a recipe my mother used. I also have some water left in my buffalo bag."

Gray took his knife out of his waistband, and cut a piece of the cake. Then, he approached Joe, and started to hand it to him.

As Joe began to reach for the cake, however, he could see a sudden change in Gray's appearance. Gray's eyes became intense once again as he raised the knife. The sun's rays were reflecting off part of the blade. The skin around his eyes was twisting the red streaks on his face.

"Be still." Gray whispered.

Joe froze in horror as Gray plunged the knife deep between his thighs.

Gray stood up holding a large snake, his knife blade stuck through its head. "Rattlesnake like warm bodies. He, probably, slept with you last night. If you had moved again, he would have bitten you."

"Yeah, right into my balls."

Gray walked away and began skinning the snake.

"We have meat today if we need it."

Joe had to smile a little. Now, he knew he had help to get back to the ranch, but in a way he would never had expected.

The old cottonwood trees were offering less shade now, and the heat of the early morning sun was once again becoming intense as Gray finished dressing Joe's right leg. "I put a piece of a tree limb against your chap, and bound it with some old rawhide I took from my breeches. It should be strong enough. I tell you, Joe, your leg is broken in two places, and it doesn't look good. I am afraid you need a doctor or a medicine man soon."

Joe moved his leg a little, and it didn't hurt nearly as much as he thought it would. "Okay, Gray, help me up."

Gray grabbed Joe's left arm and started to rise.

Joe babbled. "I've been sitting on the rocky ground so long, that it has made an imprint on my ass. It feels worse than when I have been sitting in the ranch's outhouse too long. There, those rugged pine boards around a carved toilet seat would give me splinters. Here, the ground gives me a sore ass."

As Joe stood up, he pivoted slightly on his right foot. "Got to get the feel of using the splint you made."

Gray kept his shoulder under Joe's left arm as he attempted to walk. Gray could feel Joe was gaining confidence with each step. Though Joe slipped a few times, he kept going forward until he approached the second cottonwood tree. Then he stretched out both hands, and gave it a big bear hug. He was holding on for dear life.

A stoic looking Gray lowered his eyebrows and nodded.

"Very good. Now let's try it again."

"Yeah, sure. You try it first."

"I will make you a cane. You'll walk even better."

True to Gray's word, after each attempt, Joe continued to improve. He limped, but he did walk better and better, and with less pain. The cane helped a lot.

Gray looked up at the sky. "Maybe we can get you back to your ranch before sundown?"

Joe replied, "I don't know, but I am willing to give it a try."

"Let me get my water bag and we will start out."

Joe stared at his dust-covered saddle. "What about my saddle? It was a gift from the mayor of Santa Fe for breaking in his Palomino. It's got a high arch, and has lots of silver on it, all hand carved. I can't leave it here."

Gray gave no answer.

"And where's my rifle and my whip?"

"I hid them under the leaves and dust near the trees. No one will find it."

Joe was upset. Weather worn wrinkles appeared on his brow. "That's my special Winchester!" He yelled.

"There were no bullets in the magazine, and you don't have any with you. I checked. The rifle is extra weight. Besides the rifle is safe inside its scabbard."

"No bullets?"

Joe knew he always carried bullets in his saddlebag.

"And my whip? I need that too."

Gray pointed toward the Uinta Mountains. "Two days ago I saw a ranch house near those mountains. Maybe it is your home. I hope so, but it is miles away. Yesterday, when I saw you coming up the knoll to the cottonwood trees, you were mumbling to yourself, like a crazy man. You had no idea where you were. We cannot make it, dragging a saddle and carrying a rifle and a whip. I believe I have just enough water for us to make it to that ranch."

Joe looked into his young face. Gray's eyes showed great strength and conviction. He knew then this was a strong young person who should be listened to. "Okay. You are right. Forget the saddle, and rifle. I can always get new ones."

"Let's get started."

Slowly, they meandered down the side of the mesa, Joe stumbling a couple of times, on some loose pebbles. With Gray's support, the stumbling was corrected, and they walked onward. Gray kept his eyes on the mountains that lay straight ahead, while

Joe kept his eyes focused on the ground, and where he would place his broken leg next. Progress was slow but steady.

The sun rose higher in the sky. The hard earth was heating up. It was creeping into Joe's boots. Joe thought the heat must be cooking the soles of Gray's bare feet, but he acted as if he didn't feel it.

Without notice, Gray stopped suddenly.

Joe looked up. "Why did you stop? I can go further. My leg doesn't bother me that much."

Gray looked back, and scanned the horizon. He could barely see the mesa. It was more than two miles away, and disappearing behind a haze. "Be quiet. I hear something or someone."

"Quiet? I hear nothing, but, maybe, an occasional tumbleweed rolling by."

"There it is again. It sounds like something's tingling."

Joe's hope rose. His spirits perked up as he looked back. "Now I hear it too. It sounds like a bell and it's getting closer."

Gray became afraid. "My uncle has a piebald mustang with a bell attached to its mane, but that sound was different from the one I am hearing. Before I started my journey, my uncle told me a few renegade Apaches were reported in the area. They kill anyone that gets in their way. They also love things that make a noise. We must hurry."

Gray handed the water bag to Joe.

"Take a drink of water quickly.

On the open land, there are few places to hide. We must hurry on."

Gray grabbed a piece of tumbleweed and tried to sweep away a few of their footprints as they continued on. He picked up the pace, and Joe started staggering at times, just trying to keep up. They covered a quarter of a mile, when the part of Joe's splint hit a chiseled rock, and broke. Gray grabbed Joe, and tried hard to keep him upright, but Joe was too heavy. He dropped to the ground. Gray could see sweat was covering his entire shirt. He knew his leader was exhausted.

Joe laid there, wincing in pain as a new trickle of blood ran down his chap." I think it is no use, Gray. My leg is killing me now. You go on and get some help."

"I will find some wood, and make a new splint for you."

"Look around, you dumb Indian. There is no wood in this damn hellhole. You go now. That is an order from your leader."

"So you are my leader?"

"Yeah, I guess so. But go now before that sound, whatever it is, comes closer, or I change my mind."

A stubborn Gray grabbed Joe's shirt collar, and started to pull. "What are you doing?"

"I see a large rock, not far away. It offers some shade and protection."

Joe nodded but said not a word as Gray dragged him a few yards to the rock.

Gray gave Joe the rattlesnake meat. Then he took his knife from his belt, and handed it to him. "You take it. You will need it. Eat the snake meat too. It's good for you. It will keep you alive."

Joe raised his cane in defiance. "I still have this, if those Apaches come too close."

"The cane will do you no good as a weapon. It has no spirit. Use the knife. It has spirit."

Joe took the knife, and grunted. Then he forced a weak smile as he pointed the knife in the direction of the mountains. "Get out of here, damn you!"

Gray grabbed the water bag, turned, and began to jog. He felt he could do it all day if need be. His tribal warriors were surefooted, possessed great stamina, and had lots of determination.

Joe watched Gray quickly disappear into a haze. A thought filtered through his mind. Could this be the end of the trail for me?

Chapter

3

A few late afternoon clouds were touching the peaks of the Uinta Mountains as two ranch hands stepped out of the Delta D bunkhouse. Curley, a five foot nine inch cowpoke with a short beard covering his pock marked chin, was carrying a whiskey bottle in one hand, and a wad of dollar bills in the other. Goldie, a shorter, wiry, part Mexican, part Irish man wearing a torn sombrero, was his range partner. Together they laughed and staggered as they walked across the yard toward the corral.

Goldie slapped Curley on the back and said jokingly. "Let's get out of here, and go into Bitter Wells. We'll go to Crazy Dave's Saloon, and have a few whiskeys. You know Molly loves to dance, and show off her bloomers. Maybe, we can buy her a new pair." Goldie chuckled.

Curley wasn't so sure. "I don't know. Every time we do that, I lose all my money either on the poker table, or on some whore. I might be a little drunk right now, but I know it takes a month or two of hard work moving those cows around before I see . . ." Curley raised his hand with the wad of bills, and stared at them . . . this kind of money. Maybe, I should save it. My sister back east has a friend who wants to meet me. Sister says she is cute, and wants to come out west."

"Oh, forget that stuff for now. We just finished a few hard days on the range. I will make sure you do not spend all your money, amigo. And besides, if Griff Douglas, the owner of this ranch, sees us drinking around here, he will kick both our asses out. You know how he doesn't allow drinking on the ranch. You know better too, not to stash your bottles of whiskey under your cot."

"It helps me get over all my sneezing."

"Sneezing? That's bullshit! You know it's the damn dust in the air that's being stirred up by all those dumb longhorn cattle. Keep your bandana over your nose, and you'll be okay. I promise you."

Then, the thought of a naked Molly crept into his Curley's

mind. "Are you sure you'll watch me, that you won't have to lay me across my saddle, and lead my horse back to the ranch? That I will still have money in my pockets, and not a pair of Molly's bloomers?"

Goldie grinned his reassurance, showing his one gold tooth. "Yes, I will drink very little. I will even stay next to you while you are in Molly's bedroom."

"Now, that's going a bit too far, don't you think? I want to enjoy my time with Molly, not have you hanging over me. Just see that Molly gets her money after I leave the bedroom. Okay?"

Goldie was happy. He put a wad of chewing tobacco in his mouth. "Okay, amigo. Let's saddle up and ride. And when we get a ways down the trail, please throw that damn bottle in the brush."

As both men started saddling up their mounts, they looked at each other.

"Do you hear something, Goldie?" "No, I do not."

There was no noise, just dead silence. The cattle were quiet, and the new colts the owner had bought yesterday, were in the corral standing, but not moving at all. Duke, the owner's dog, a large German shepherd, usually patrolled the areas around the main house, barking at an occasional jackrabbit, but he was nowhere to be seen.

A soft breeze developed, and caused a loose board on the outhouse door to groan.

"You happy now? You hear your noise now, my amigo."

"Yeah, I guess you're right. Nuthin' wrong with quietness,

I guess. It's just unusual not to hear something."

Goldie stated back. "All the buckaroos are either with the owner, searching for Joe Lundy, or sleeping in the bunkhouse. Let's get out of here while we can."

Both cowboys mounted their horses. As Curley shook the reins, his horse raised its forelegs, and snorted.

Goldie saw Dancer's lips roll back. "What's wrong with your horse?" "He senses danger. I see him act like this whenever a rattlesnake is nearby, or some damn Indian. He hates Indians ever since a brave hit him with a tomahawk."

"What Indian?"

Dancer was very agitated, his hooves stomping the earth. Curley patted Dancer's neck. "Easy boy. Easy boy. Everything's all right."

Dancer seemed to settle down a little.

"We were at the Fort Charles rodeo. Dancer started prancing and kicking up some dust. That dust hit one of those lazy Indians that always hung around the fort. The Indian threw his tomahawk and it hit Dancer right on the ass. Dancer never forgot it."

Curley and Goldie scanned all the open land beyond the corral.

Goldie spoke. "I see nothing but an eagle soaring above the mountains. Let's get out of here."

"You are probably right. It must have been a snake that has slithered away."

Curley gave a final glance, and started to pull on the left rein when he heard another noise. It came from the east side of the corral. "Did you hear that?"

"Si, it sounded like a low moan."

Curley became tense. "Maybe it was a cry for help."

Goodie stood up in his stirrups, and searched the rugged landscape again. This time, he pointed straight ahead. "Now, I see someone over there, waving something. He just stumbled, and fell down."

Curley saw it too, and responded. "It's an Indian. I saw the buffalo water bag he was waving."

"Let's go help him."

Goodie was perturbed. "Go help him? He is just a lonely savage. A vermin. We kill vermin around here, don't we?"

"He is a human being. He needs our help!"

Goldie argued. "He might be one of those Apache renegades that are supposed to be in the area. They're sneaky bastards. They kill for no good reason." Goldie paused. "And remember, Curley, Molly with those beautiful white legs, is waiting for us.

Curley would have none of it. He yanked the reins hard, and dug his spurs into Dancer's side. Dancer resisted at first, but conceded to his will. Together, they headed around the corral. Goldie, reluctantly, followed behind, spitting a mouthful of tobacco juice at the ground.

A small cloud of dust rose up as Curley pulled back on the reins. He could see a young boy lying, facedown, his hand clinching an empty buffalo water bag. Curley dismounted Dancer, rushed to the Indian's side, and turned him over, while Goldie remained in his saddle.

Curley looked at Goldie, "This boy is unconscious, and needs of water. Throw me your canteen."

Goldie put his hand over his canteen. "I don't want any Indian putting his lips on my canteen. Leave him here. And why don't use your own canteen?"

"My canteen is empty. I forgot to fill it. Now throw me yours." Goldie shook his head.

Curley pulled out his revolver, and pointed it at his partner. "Goldie, throw me that damn canteen, or you'll be missing that prized tooth of yours. You wouldn't look good in Bitter Wells without it, would you?

Reluctantly, Goldie untied the strap holding the canteen to the saddle, and threw it at Curley. The canteen was heading toward the boy's head until Curley caught it in midair.

A gruff Goldie sneered. "When we get back to bunk house, you wash that canteen real good, inside and out! You hear!"

Curley paid no attention. He lifted the boy's head, and poured a little water into his mouth. Next, he took his bandana, poured water over all of it, and placed it on the boy's forehead. Curley spoke to Goldie as he continued to pour more water into the boy's mouth. "This boy is from the mountain Ute tribe. See the symbol on the boy's buffalo bag? They are good, peaceful people. We have never had any trouble with them. In fact, I haven't seen a Ute in years. I wonder what he is doing around here."

"Probably trying to steal some of our horses, I'd bet." "Don't be so spiteful. He didn't do anything to you." "Not yet."

"Indians are all the same. They stampeded my cattle all over my corn fields, and stole my favorite horse."

Curley had to respond. "You told me that was a long time ago in Mexico. And I seem to remember you telling me you got your horse back."

Goldie turned his head, and looked away.

The boy started to revive. His face was covered in dust. Some of the water had mixed with the dust, and formed globules of mud around his lips. His eyelids slowly opened. He looked at the cowboy, who had his head cradled in his arms.

"Where am I?" he spoke in English. Both cowboys were amazed. "You speak good English?" Curly said.

"Yes. White man teaches me."

"You are close to the Douglas Ranch. We heard you cry out, and watched you fall down. My name is Curley, and this is my partner, Goldie. What is your name?"

"My name is Gray." He squirmed a little, and then tried to get up, but it was no use.

"Gray, relax. You need plenty of rest, water, and food. I will lay you across my saddle, and will walk Dancer back to our bunkhouse. There you can rest."

Curley threw the canteen back to Goldie. Then he lifted Gray, and laid him across the saddle. A partly conscious Gray started to speak. "Curley, I have come to get help for my friend."

Goldie pulled hard on his sombrero. "Not another Indian?"

"Pay no mind to Goldie. Who is your friend?"

"Joe."

"Joe who?" Gray started to drift off.

"Do you mean Joe Lundy?"

"Yes. Please help him." Curley was stunned.

"We have a search party out looking for him. Where is he?"

Slipping into unconsciousness, Gray spoke. "He's south, a ways back, maybe, a half day's trip by horse. He is resting next to a rock. He needs a doctor bad."

"Thanks, Gray. After we get back to the bunkhouse, I'll get the few guys in the bunk house together, and we will find him."

Curley led his horse with Gray draped over the saddle, back to the ranch house. A sad and disappointed Goldie followed some distance behind.

Amy, Griff Douglas's pretty, little wife, with blondish hair tied up in a bun, heard all the commotion. First, it was sound of the horses' hooves, and voices of men chattering about something. Then, she heard the bunkhouse door slam shut, and a lot of raucous noises. It sounded to her like a wildcat was tearing up the place.

She placed her knitting on the side table, and rose from her rocking chair. She opened the parlor door, and peered outside. She could see a bunch of the cowhands, half clothed, racing around the corral next to the barn, trying to grab their saddles and their horses. In the process, a lot of dust was being kicked up. She could hear a growing cacophony of loud voices and sounds; people who were in great need to do something, but what?

Through all the dust being stirred up, she recognized one of them, and shouted. "Curley, what is going on out here? Why are all our cowhands in a hurry to leave?"

Curley walked over to Amy. "Madam, Goldie and I found an

Indian boy lying on the ground, on the other side of the corral. He was very weak, and partly conscious. We gave him some water, and brought him back to the bunkhouse. He told us he was a friend of Joe Lundy, our missing cowhand. Just now, Goldie and I put the boy on my cot, and told everybody what the boy had said. What you are seeing is a mad scramble to find Joe before dark.

"You say you have an Indian boy lying on your cot? I hope he is not one of those roving Apaches bands the whole town is talking about?"

"No, Mrs. Douglas, he is a mountain Ute. They are very friendly people. How he got here is a mystery. He is very dehydrated, and weak, as I have said."

"Curley, you and Goldie carry the boy into my house, and put him on one of the cots in the back room."

Curley wondered. "Are you sure you want to do that? He had paint on his face. It looks like war paint to me, but I am no expert."

"Joe Lundy is an expert on Indians, and if he got along with this boy, the boy must be okay. Besides, I was a nurse in the Civil War, and took care of a lot of soldiers on both sides. Bring him over now."

"Yes, madam." As Curley started for the bunkhouse, he motioned for Goldie to come to him. An indifferent Goldie dismounted and met Curley at the door. "Mrs. Douglas wants you and me to carry the Indian boy to the back room in her house."

"Why me? Can't you get somebody else?"

"No, she said she wanted you to do it. Besides, all the cowhands are off looking for Joe."

Goldie looked dejected. "Can we still go to Crazy Dave's?"

"No, I'm afraid not. It would not be right to leave Mrs. Douglas all alone Besides, I am sobering up fast."

A few hours passed. Twilight was coming on. There was no sign of the cowhands bringing Joe Lundy home. Mrs. Douglas, in the meantime, had washed Gray's face, hands, and feet, and had fed him a cup of her homemade chicken noodle soup. Gray rested, and waited. He knew he had found some new friends, but his thoughts were on his leader, Joe Lundy.

Gray felt a slight movement in the cot. It was so slight most people would have never notice it. Gray's muscles tensed as the gentle shake continued. Something or someone was pounding the ground. Then, his ears detected another sound. Both sounds continued, and they were getting closer. Then, Gray recognized the second sound. It was the tingling of a bell. He was sure it was the same bell that Joe and he had heard before.

Gray fought hard to stand up. Amy heard him, dropped her knitting once again, and hurried back into the room. "Gray, you get back in bed right now. You are in no condition to do anything. Do as I say or I will get Curley! He knows how to handle you."

"Madam, I hear a sound, and it is close by. Joe and I heard it earlier. It's the sound of a bell, one that I have never heard before today. It could be one of those Apaches."

"You get back in bed, and I will get my rifle." "Rifle?"

"Yes, my rifle. I bet I can shoot better than most of the cowhands around here. Got my training in the action at Bull Run. I can shoot the eyes out of a prairie dog at two hundred yards. No renegade Indian is coming in here."

Gray lay back down on the cot as Amy grabbed the rifle off the parlor wall above the mantle, and hurried outside. Curley and Goldie who were coming from the bunkhouse greeted her.

Amy spoke. "What are you doing out here?"

Curley replied, "Someone has to mind the ranch, don't they? Besides, we heard a bell somewhere out there on the prairie. We were going to check it out." Curley stared at the rifle in Amy's hand. "What are you doing with that?"

"Gray said he and Joe heard that bell earlier today. He doesn't know what kind of bell it was, but he was afraid the Apaches might have one. I got my rifle, just in case, it I would need it."

"Put that rifle back well you had it. We will take care of this. No harm will come to you, I promise."

"Okay, if you say so."

Amy started to walk into her house when she, too, heard the sound of the bell. It was not a constant sound, but it was becoming louder. Curley and Goldie ran to their horses already saddled, and climbed aboard. Amy grabbed her rifle, and aimed it at the corner of the bunkhouse. If that bell came around the corner, she was ready to fire. Curley and Goldie raced their horses around the bunkhouse to face any challenge.

Time seemed to stand still. Amy was not used to holding an eight pound rifle for so long. Her arms gave out, and she lowered her weapon. She heard no sounds from Curley or Goldie, but she still heard that damn bell. What was it?

She stood there on the porch, the door wide open, when a soft breeze developed. The coolness it brought was a welcome sign of relief. She walked over to a rocker on the porch, and sat down, her rifle resting on her lap.

She waited.

Around the corner of the bunkhouse Curley and Goldie appeared, riding very slowly. Each had a broad grin on his face. She stood up and dropped her rifle as they led a visitor up to the ranch house. It was an old prospector leading a ragged looking donkey. Joe Lundy with his rifle in his left hand was sitting on his saddle atop the donkey. There was a cowbell attached to the donkey's neck. It rang once as the prospector stopped the animal.

Curley and Goldie dismounted as Amy walked toward Joe. "How are you doing?"

Joe nodded. "Much better since this prospector found me."

"I am sure happy to see you are safe. You had all of us scared." "Madam, an Indian named Gray saved my life. He sent smoke

signals, which this man saw, and found me half dead. I owe both of them my life and my thanks."

Under a worn floppy felt hat stood a gray bearded prospector. He was holding the reins of the donkey. "My name is Elias, madam, and this is my best friend, Penny. We've been prospecting in the mountains around here for more than ten years and Penny has always been by my side."

"Thanks for your help, Elias."

But Amy was surprised too. "You are the only one I know who is prospecting in these mountains these days. Did you find anything?"

Elias pulled out of his shirt pocket a large nugget of gold. "This is the first one I found ten years ago. It was lying in a mountain spring. Pretty thing, isn't it? I haven't found any more since then, but Penny and I keep on looking."

Joe spoke up. "Madam, my right hand is badly sprained, and my right leg is broken in two places. Both an Indian boy and Elias have tried to keep the leg well enough for a doctor to fix. Elias put an old ointment on the fractures to stop the bleeding, but it still hurts like hell."

Amy tried to smile. "Gray, the Indian boy you mentioned is inside on a cot. He was very dehydrated, but I am nursing him back to health."

"Is Gray well enough for me to see him?"

"Sure is, but first you need to get settled in. I have an extra cot in the back room. You can keep Gray company after I fix your wounds. The doctor in Bitter Wells is out of town for a week or more, so I will have to be his substitute."

"Substitute?"

"Yes, but don't worry. . ."

Both Curley and Goldie chimed in. "Yes, we know. She was in the Civil War, cutting off arms and legs. We've heard it all before."

Amy became snippety. "Okay you wise Asses, bring Joe inside, and bring me a bucket of hot water, and a dirty knife."

"Dirty knife?" Curley asked.

Amy looked at him, square in the eye and winked.

"The knife is in case I have to cut out your tongue. Oh yes, I smell that terrible booze both of you have been drinking. Clean yourselves up before my husband returns."

Curley and Goldie carefully pulled Joe off the saddle and carried him inside.

Amy looked at Elias. "Again, my personal thanks for saving one of our best cowhands. Why not stay overnight? I'll find a place for you inside the house."

"No, thanks Maam. But Penny and I would like to stay in your barn for the night. We will leave in the morning."

"Well, that's fine, but I do want you to come for dinner. I am making chicken and dumplings and black eyed peas."

"Thank you Maam, that sounds awfully good." Elias started to turn to lead Penny toward the barn. He stopped and said, "Madam, what should I do with his saddle, his rifle, and whip?"

"Put them on the porch next to my chair."

"Yes, madam." Elias paused. "Oh, by the way, I found a piece of a cocklebur buried under the saddle. You know it can dig through the saddle blanket and make a horse do funny things."

"Thanks for telling me about that."

Mrs. Douglas entered the house while Elias took Joe's saddle off Penny, and carried it to the porch. In the morning he would head back to get Penny's pack saddle he had to leave on the trail.

Sundown was approaching fast.

Amy Douglas hurried from her sewing room holding a box containing scissors, a sharp knife, needles, and strong thread. She saw Joe grimace in pain as Curley and Goldie lay him down on a cot. Joe, in turn, noticed Gray sitting on the edge of his cot: his sunken eyes focused on him. He could see Gray's determination to know what was going to happen to his leader.

Joe smiled.

"Howdy partner. How are . . .?"

A sudden pain shot up his leg, stopping him from speaking.

Gray tried to stand, and come to Joe's aid, but a determined Amy pushed him back onto the cot.

"You stay on that cot, you hear. You are in no shape to be moving around."

Gray bowed to her wishes and lay down on his cot, but he did turn on his side, so he could watch was going to happen next.

"You can say howdy to Joe. That's all. Tomorrow both of you should be much better. Right now, Joe is a very sick man who needs all my help."

Amy was small in height, but strong in leadership skills. She could be quite harsh when the need arose. Gray seemed to sense it was not a good time to test her demands.

"Howdy, Joe."

"Howdy, Gray. I'm glad." Joe coughed "to see you made it."

"Thanks."

Amy turned her attention back to Joe. He looked quite pale, his eyes not focusing. She knew from her Civil War experiences what would have to be done.

"Goldie, you'll find some clean towels under the kitchen sink, bring them here. Oh, I'll need your bandana too. Curly, you bring me one of the bottles of booze you always keep hidden. Now hurry!"

Goldie headed toward the kitchen while Curley marched out the front door. Curley was annoyed. How did Mrs. Douglas know about my booze; he wondered? He had kept them so well hidden! That was his private stock. Nobody should know about it, except maybe Goldie!

Amy gently removed the bloodstained chaps from both legs, leaned over, and with her knife started cutting through the leather strips wrapped around Joe's right leg. She carefully removed two tree limbs that were acting as splints, and took a cursory look at the wound. A terrible smell greeted her and spread throughout the room. Gray and Goldie turned their heads. She wanted to shake her head in disbelief, but she didn't want Joe to see her do it. The wound appeared to be much worse than she had anticipated.

"What's that terrible smell?" Joe had caught a strong whiff too. "It's the smell of an infection," Amy replied.

She knew she needed to do a complete inspection, so she took her scissors and cut straight up the right trouser leg to just, above the knee, and then cut across both sides of it. She spread out the two parts of denim trouser. With great interest, she examined the wound, finding some infection and rotting flesh. The stench was almost unbearable. The shinbone was discolored and broken twice. A small piece of bone was missing too.

She stood erect, and looked Joe straight in the eye. "You have a bad case of gangrene, I am sad to say. Nothing can be done to save your right leg. It is imperative I cut off your leg just above the knee as soon as possible. I make no promises, but that should save your life. Since the doctor is out of town for God knows how long, I am your only hope.

Joe replied with a soft smile. "Do what you have to do. I'm ready. Just let me puff on a cigarette for a minute, so I can forget that smell."

Joe reached for a carved elk handle sticking out of his pants pocket. "And give this knife to Gray. It's his."

Amy nodded as she took the knife and handed it to Gray.

Goldie held the towels under his left arm, pulled a rolled cigarette out of his dusty shirt pocket with his right hand, lit it with a finger match, and handed it to Joe.

Amy smiled. "What a great soldier Joe would have made in the Civil War. Some of our best men I had to tie down. They had become delirious with the thought of losing an arm or a leg. You would think I was cutting off their peckers." Amy paused. She felt a little embarrassed.

"Oh, please forgive my bad language, boys."

Goldie placed the towels, and his bandana on the end of the cot. Curley came waltzing through the doorway. He still seemed a little reluctant to give away one of his prized bottles. Amy grabbed a hold of it, uncapped it, and handed it to Joe. She raised her voice. "Have a ball. Drink all of it. Pretend you are whoopin' it up in Dave's saloon, having fun with the ladies. Everyone around here does it on payday."

All who were standing in the room began looking at each other.

How did Amy know so much about their activities?

She looked up. "Okay, okay. So I hear things, and I can put two and two together."

Joe tried to laugh, but couldn't. Amy was one smart lady, he realized.

"Joe, after you have finished that bottle, I have another one for you."

Joe's eyebrows rose.

"No, it's not booze, it is a bottle of ether. I saved it after the Civil War was over. I thought I might have a use for it someday, and I see that someday is now. If the booze doesn't knock you out, the ether will. It's powerful stuff. So as fast as you can finish that bottle, the faster I can take care of your leg."

A somber Amy turned to face Curley. "Go to the blacksmith shop, and bring me the small saw hanging on the wall. It's the one with a lot of notches on the handle. I might be adding one more today."

Amy looked up at everyone.

"Just in case any of you don't know, those notches are every person that I have had to amputate an arm or leg, and who have survived. Don't bother counting them all, Curley, but please do heat the blade. I want it as sterile as possible."

"Yes, madam."

Amy had another thought. This amputation could be a real bleeder. "Goldie, get a tin cup full of sawdust from the wood shed, and bring it here."

"Si madam.

As Goldie walked away, Amy could see Curley had not left the room. "Curley, bring me another bottle of booze.

My husband will understand. Later, we will be celebrating the success of this operation, and the start of Joe's recovery."

The forlorn cowboy lowered his head and muttered something as he walked out the front door.

"She wants another bottle!"

A weak Joe was passing out fast.

Amy stared at her patient, and questioned herself. "I might not need the ether after all."

She was about to begin sawing when she heard a dog barking. A group of riders pulled up to the hitching post, jumped off their horses, and raced through the open doorway.

"Howdy, hon. Watcha been doin'? Wow! What's that terrible smell?" There was no reply.

It was Griff Douglas who stepped into the spare room, and noticed a person on a cot. A ring of cigarette smoke still hovered above his head.

Duke came up to Griff's side, and began barking. Without looking down, Griff issued an order. "Duke, get out on the back porch now." The dog left the room, his tail between his legs, while Griff continued to stare at Amy, and the man on the cot. "Is that Joe Lundy? We've been looking for him all day. How is he doing? How did he get there?"

"He's lost a lot of blood and water. His right leg is broken in two places, and there is gangrene in the leg to boot." Amy had stated the facts rather coldly.

"Is he going to make it?" Griff's face started to show increasing concern. "You know he is one of the best cattle drivers I have ever had."

Amy pointed to Joe's leg. "Yes, I know he is a good cowhand, but I don't know about his life." She steered Griff away. I "have to get to work right now, while Joe is unconscious. I am going to saw off his leg, so please excuse me. I'll tell you more later."

Amy turned her attention back to the patient, while Griff repeated to his men what his wife had said, and then ushered all of them out of the house.

As Amy started sawing, she yelled. "Griff, there is chicken noodle soup on the stove. Help yourself. Supper will be late."

"Thanks. I'll have some after I wash up, and that smell goes away."

Gray watched with great interest as Amy started sawing Joe's leg off just above the knee but did save some of the extra skin. She packed the end of the stump with sawdust, grabbed a cloth, and held it tight against the bloody stump for several minutes. When she was sure there was sufficient clotting in the ends of the arteries and veins, she removed the bloody cloth, and began to carefully sew the extra skin together over the stump. She proceeded to tightly wrap a towel around the stump. Next, she wrapped Goldie's bandana around the towel, took both ends, and tied them in a knot. She knew the pressure on the leg would help prevent any blood clots from forming in Joe's bloodstream.

"Goldie. Bury Joe's leg somewhere out behind the bunkhouse. Buried it deep so the coyotes can't get to it."

"Si, madam." Goldie agreed, but was not happy. Why did he get the dirty work all the time?

Then, she examined Joe's right shoulder and hand. Both were severely bruised, but not broken. She could see the nerves and tendons in the hand were ruined, and could not be repaired. She knew the hand would be of little use to him.

The shoulder, however, was a different story. Amy asked Curley to grab a jar of horse liniment she kept in her cupboard. She knew a thorough massage over the sprain each day would do the trick.

In a short time, she was picking up her tools, and hurrying back to the kitchen. She knew making a late supper would keep her busy, and away from her favorite pastime: knitting. The men would have to wait, she mused. A woman can only do so much in a day.

Gray continued to lie on his side staring at his silent leader. He believed Joe would get well soon. The vision he had while sitting in the cottonwood tree would see to it. He was sure of it. Later, Gray would help him to get up and walk again, maybe even learn to shoot his rifle. Then, they could go find a Gray Owl feather, hopefully a big one.

Gray's eyes closed on that expectation,

"Good fixings, Mrs. Douglas," Goldie said. While the others agreed, Goldie raised his hand. "Pass me a couple of those delicious buttermilk biscuits."

Amy Douglas prided herself with how good supper had turned out. Sometimes, haste doesn't make waste after all. She sighed. When you have six hungry men sitting at the table, it can get pretty hectic keeping them occupied and well fed.

Curley tried to show his concern. "Mrs. Douglas, will Joe be pullin' through?" He liked Joe, but deep inside he really was worried he might have to give away more of his private stock.

Amy could read his mind. "Curley, if Joe gets through the night, there is a fifty-fifty chance he will live a long time. It is one of the worst wounds I have ever seen. We just have to wait and see." Amy winked. "Try praying, why don't you!"

Amy grabbed Curley's other bottle of whiskey off the top shelf of the hutch and handed it to Griff. He stood up, uncapped it, and raised it high in the air as Amy opened the hutch doors.

"Don't bother with any glasses, honey. This is a cowboy's toast for having Joe back with us, and to my wife, Amy, who is trying to save his life." A rousing cheer went up from the men.

Griff looked in the prospector's direction. "I want to personally thank you, Elias, and your donkey for carrying Joe back to our ranch.

Another cheer.

Elias smiled, the candlelight revealing he had just two front teeth. Griff took a swig and gave it to Rusty, the foreman. Rusty took a swig, and then passed it to the next man, and so on.

It was after nine o'clock at night, and Curley agreed to help with the dishes. Griff told Gus and Rusty what he wanted the men living in the bunkhouse to do the next day: move the younger longhorns into a separate corral; get your gear ready for the yearly cattle drive to the railhead; fix the leak on the barn roof, and repair the wheel on his wife's buckboard. Griff would take care of the two new colts he had bought two days ago at an auction.

Everyone arose from their chair at the same time, wiping their mouths once more on Amy's linen napkins.

All the men started to walk out the door in single file, when Gray came rushing out of his room.

"Mrs. Douglas," he called.

Griff intercepted him as the others looked on.

"What's your problem? And who the hell are you anyway?"

Amy saw the commotion, and stepped in front of her husband. "I forgot to tell you.

This is the young boy who saved Joe's life. His name is Gray" Amy raised her voice.

"I think he has something to say, so please listen." "Oh, all right. What is it?"

Gray was afraid at first of the big man who towered over him. Out of nervousness, Gray tried to answer back in his native tongue.

"Stop the gibberish. Talk English, boy!"

Gray swallowed hard. "I heard a very soft noise that most people would never hear. Hunting with my uncle taught me what to listen for. We would find many deer that way."

"Get on with it. What's this all about?" "Please listen Griff." Amy pleaded.

"I heard a soft noise outside my window. I looked out and saw three Indians sneaking into your barn. I am sure of it."

"Three Indians?"

"Yes, I am sure of it. I think they are Apaches."

Griff's face turned red with anger. "I bet those thievin' bastards are after my new horses." He turned toward his men and Amy. "Gus, you and Rusty go out the back door, while Goldie and Curley go with me out the front door. Have your guns ready." Griff looked at his wife. "You stay here, my love, and grab your rifle just in case."

"Elias and Gray, you stay inside with the Mrs."

It was a full moon with few clouds to hide its light. Each man did exactly as he had been told. A bit of a shadow appeared on one of the corral posts, and then another. Curley saw the shadow. It was a person holding the mane of one of Griff's horses. He was trying to sneak out the far side of the corral. Curley took careful aim and fired.

The person dropped to the ground a dying moan could be heard. The horse moved to the other side of the corral.

Suddenly, the barn doors swung open and two more Indians bolted out. They were riding bareback on two horses, and whooping it up. They galloped straight across to the other side of the corral, and jumped over a couple of wooden rails. Into the dim moonlight, they faded away fast. Everyone could hear the sound of a tingling bell.

Griff went into the tool shed, lit a torch and began to look everywhere. After a short search he said to the others. It looks like the only thing they took were my two old horses. They were two old mares I didn't know what to do with, anyway.

As Griff walked across the corral, he thought aloud. "Let's check out that Indian. You know we haven't had any Indians around here in years. All of a sudden, we have had four of them. What's the hell going on?"

Curley rolled the Indian over. Griff held the torch close to the body, so everyone could see. It was an Indian boy, maybe, fifteen or sixteen years old. He was mostly skin and bones with tattooed markings covering his body. There were no weapons of importance, just a crude tomahawk.

"Gus, bring me that Indian boy that's in my house." "Right away."

A minute later, Gus and Gray stood next to Griff as he held the torch over the dead Indian. "Do you know who this boy is?"

Gray did not have to look long. He knew the markings on the body. "Yes. I do. He is a member of an isolated tribe of Chiricahua Apaches who have been raiding my people living on Hallow Mountain, and they keep stealing our food and horses."

"Thanks Gray. You can go back inside. Goldie, you and Gus give this fellow a decent burial over in the south fork. Come tomorrow, Rusty and I will go after the other two Apaches."

At first, Goldie did not like the idea of having to bury the Indian. But as he thought some more about it, a smile appeared on his face. This was like a small payback for all the grief those vermin did to him and his family in Mexico years ago.

Chapter

5

The morning sun was starting to climb above the Uinta mountain range as Griff and Rusty stopped their horses at a fork in the trail. They had been riding for the last few hours following hoof prints in the dirt. Rusty dropped the burned out torch he was carrying, stood up in the stirrups, looked around, and then spoke. "Boss, how are we ever going to find those damn Apaches? Which part of the fork do we take? We've been following the horses' hoof prints for quite a while, but now you can see those hoof prints have disappeared on this hard ground. Which trail do we follow?" Rusty was concerned. He was anxious to return to the ranch to make sure all the chores Griff had asked for, were being done.

He shook his Stetson hat. "If Joe were here, it would be no problem. He's good at tracking anything."

Griff stared straight ahead. "I'll let the nose do it." "Nose? Whose nose?"

Griff had firmness in his voice. "Duke's nose! That is whose! He can follow a smell better than the best hound dog I ever had back East in ol' Kentucky. I think he must have some bloodhound in him. Sometimes, he'll even point his tail like a hunting dog too. I'd bet he could find a needle in a haystack, if I let him."

Rusty wasn't quite sure what he was hearing. "Duke didn't find Joe yesterday, did he?"

"No, that's true, but I didn't put a piece of Joe's clothes under his nose either. We all figured Joe was somewhere close to the ranch. This time I put the blanket that had covered one of the stolen horses under Duke's nose. I tell ya that scent is locked in his brain. He'll find those horses. I'm sure of it, and we will get those damn Indians too."

A dumbstruck Rusty had to ask. "Hound dogs take off in a flash, yelping their heads off. If Duke does those things, he'll scare them off."

"Duke knows better. He knows to stay by my side until I give him the word. He makes no sounds, and stays within eyesight. It's been hours since we left the ranch. I know Duke must be ready."

Griff turned in his saddle and looked down at Duke. "How are you going to smell those thievin' bastards sitting there on your ass?

Duke's ears perked up, his eyes staring at his master.

Griff waved his arm forward and spoke in a stern voice.

"Go. Go. Find those horses."

Duke was off like a shot. He took the right fork. Griff and Rusty quickly followed.

The trail was serpentine in nature, and seemed to be headed higher into the mountains. Eventually, it turned into an arid, dusty one. It was causing Duke to sneeze a lot, but he wasn't about to give up. Various size boulders began to line the trail. Strange markings were painted on a few of them. On his right, Rusty noticed the skull of a buffalo stuck on a pole, painted in red and white colors.

"Boss, what does that skull mean? Are we entering some kind of a trap?"

Rusty and Griff slowed their horses to a trot, then pulled them to an abrupt stop.

Griff said, "I don't know, but I do see ahead of us a lot of boulders on both sides of the trail, and there is only a narrow pass to get between them."

The boss started scanning the entire area. "There could be many Apaches hiding in those boulders."

"Maybe we should not go any further?" Rusty was strong of heart, but didn't like facing the unknown. He was becoming quite nervous.

Griff thought for a moment as he scanned the area one more time. He noticed Duke's tail was pointing in a direction. He removed his bandana from his neck, and held it in the wind. A breeze was blowing the bandana toward his left side. Rusty watched, waiting for his boss's next move.

"I'd guess they are hiding downwind so they can smell the white man first. Since the wind is coming from the right side, it means they have to be in the boulders on our left side," said the boss.

Griff's horse was becoming a little nervous. Griff pulled hard on the reins. He knew his palomino, Stoney did not like Indians. He called for his dog. "Duke. Come back here."

Duke lowered his tail and walked back to Griff's horse. He waited patiently for his owner's next command.

Griff leaned over in Rusty's direction and spoke in a softer voice. "Take your rope and . . ." He pointed to the right side of the trail. "Grab two of those dried out bushes, and twist the middle of your rope a few times around each one of them."

A puzzled Rusty climbed down from his horse. He walked over to two large bushes, yanked them out of the soil, and then twisted the middle of his rope around one, and then the other.

"That'll do just fine. Now, when I tell you, you give one end of the rope to Duke. You hold on to the other end, real tight."

"What's next? A hoedown? Rusty was mystified, but never mistrusted his boss's moves.

Griff stood up in the stirrups, and surveyed the area one last time He saw no signs of Indians. He tested the wind with his bandana once again. A steadier breeze with an occasional gust was coming across the trail, and hitting the boulders on the left side.

"When I give the command, Duke will walk up the trail until the rope is taunt."

Griff looked at Duke and then pointed to the rope in Rusty's hand. "Duke, get the rope." Duke obeyed, and walked over to Rusty, sank his canines into the end of the rope, and then waited. Griff looked up the trail and waved his hand. "Now go, go. Pull hard."

At once, Duke began walking backward straightening out the rope; the bushes were being drug through large piles of dust and dirt lining the left side of the trail.

Griff looked at Rusty. "Now shake that rope as hard as you can.

Duke thinks it's a game, and he will help you by shaking his end too."

Huge plumes of irritating dust and dirt particles began to rise higher into the air, and started to cover the boulders closest to them. Visibility was becoming less and less. A few gusts came, and carried the dust even higher and higher over the tallest boulder. It was filling every nock and cranny just as Griff had hoped it would.

"Keep shaking that rope. You'll be seeing something soon."

Griff tied his bandana around his face much like a stagecoach bandit, and started toward the nearest boulder. "Rusty, I am going around the back of these two boulders and climb up. Don't stop shaking the rope until I yell. We'll get those Indian thieves right quick."

Rusty nodded while he kept shaking the rope. Soon, Griff disappeared behind the wall of dust.

Griff placed his left boot in the first crevice he found, and then the other boot in the next higher one. He carefully worked his way up through the cracks in the boulder until he had almost reached the top when he heard coughing and wheezing. He drew his revolver. The two Indian boys never saw him.

"Hands up." Griff yelled. Two Indian boys were startled and tried to fade away into the dust. One boy threw his crude tomahawk at him. It missed. Griff fired two shots over their heads.

"Stop you thieving' bastards or I will put a bullet in each one of your hearts."

The two Indians boys froze. Griff yelled to Rusty to stop the dust. Visibility increased rapidly. He motioned with his revolver the direction he wanted the Indian boys to go. They understood. The dust was settling as Griff and his captives worked their way down the front face of the boulder. Drops of blood were oozing out of captives' mouths. They were chewing something.

At the bottom Rusty took some rawhide pieces out of his saddlebag and tied their hands behind their backs. He noticed the blood too.

He looked at Griff. "Did you hit them?"

Griff shook his head a little from side to side. "What do you want to do with our prisoners?"

Griff climbed up on his horse, and looked ahead at the narrowing trail. "Rusty, I remember Joe Lundy telling me about a narrow trail he found that led to Hallow Mountain. This could be it. That Indian boy back on the ranch, Gray, told us his tribe lives around here. Since these Indian boys have been raiding his tribe, why don't we let his tribe pronounce their sentences?"

"Sounds like a good idea to me."

"Oh, by the way, that buffalo skull you saw? The Indians are telling us there are no more buffaloes left in this area. It's telling us it was stupid white man's fault."

Rusty coiled the rope, put it on the saddle, and mounted his horse. He had his horse nudge the Indian boys forward. One Indian boy turned away, disobeying the rider. Duke left Griff's side, and faced the boy with a dangerous snarl. Griff could see the fear in the boy's eyes as he turned around, and continued to walk ahead.

Rusty smiled. "I see Duke takes no crap from anybody."

"Yeah, an old trainer in town taught him well. He did a good thing. Duke has been my trusted friend for six years now."

Rusty was puzzled. "Boss, how did you know that those Indian boys would be on the first two boulders and not the bigger ones where the trail gets really narrow?"

"I figured this way. Most people would be on guard for an ambush where the trail is the narrowest. If I was a smart Indian and wanted to ambush somebody, I would do it before they ever got to the bigger boulders. It would take them by complete surprise. When I saw Duke's pointed tail, I knew I was right."

Rusty was relieved. He smiled. "And you were right as usual, boss." Griff shook his bandana, and wiped his face. He was beginning to have thoughts of home. "I wonder how Joe is doing? I hope he makes it. He's been a big part of my cattle business. He saved my prized bulls, I was told."

"Joe is strong. Your wife will take good care of him." Rusty reassured him.

"Okay." "Let's get these Indian boys to Hallow Mountain as quickly as we can."

Griff and Rusty made their horses set a faster pace. The Indian boys didn't like it, but had no choice. As they passed the narrowest part of the trail, Griff and Rusty saw the remains of Griff's stolen horses. They were dead, lying on their sides. Chunks of their flesh had been removed.

Now, Griff and Rusty knew where the blood on the Indian boys' mouths had come from, and what they were chewing.

The going was slow, but steady.

"Rusty, we should be coming to the top of Hallow Mountain soon. Do you know how it got its name?"

"No, I don't," Rusty said as he pushed the Apache boys to walk faster.

"The chief of the Northern Utes had a baby boy who was dying. The baby would not drink any of his mother's milk. The chief was worried that he was going to lose his only son. He had the shaman ask the gods for help. The shaman carried the baby in his arms to the very top of this mountain. The grieving chief and his wife followed.

Standing on top of the mountain, the shaman raised the baby above his head and said a prayer and a chant. Out of one of the many crevasses appeared a very old woman. She began walking toward them. She was chanting too. On her head was the head of a coyote with its pelt draping down her back. She showed no emotion, but took the baby and placed its mouth on her only tit. Miraculously, the baby began to suck, and his health quickly improved. The mysterious lady gave the baby back to its mother, and then disappeared back into one of the crevasses. From that time on, that lady is known as Coyote Woman Does Good."

The chief was so impressed that he claimed the mountain to be "Holy." The baby grew up and became a famous chief who led his tribe to many victories. Over the years, the mountain took on a respected place for all who seek guidance, and it became known as Hallow Mountain. The few white people that dare to go there, say they find joy and enlightenment like no other place. Maybe I can get Amy to go to the mountain with me someday."

Rusty had one question. "Griff, did the baby suck on the woman's left tit or the right one?"

"I can see you were not listening to me. The woman had only one tit, right in the middle of her breast. Okay?"

Both men looked at each other and chuckled aloud.

Around a flat bend in the trail, just below the top of the mountain was a small group of teepees. There were kids of all ages running around, playing a game using a stick and the skull of a rabbit as a ball. The chief had already been made aware of four people coming up the trail. He had donned his finest loincloth and was stepping out of the largest teepee when he noticed the two Apache boys that had been raiding his camp. He studied their movements for a few seconds, and then looked up at the two men sitting on their horses. He stared, wondering why these two white men would come this far up the mountain.

Rusty patted his horse's neck while Griff tried using sign language.

It was no use. He didn't know how.

Griff looked over all the tribe members grouped around the chief, and asked, "Does anyone speak English?" He repeated his question. "Don't be afraid. I need to talk to your chief."

A few seconds of silence passed. Then a teenage girl spoke in a very demure voice. "I speak some English."

The chief looked quizzically at the girl. A frown appeared on his forehead, but he said nothing.

"Good. Would you tell the chief we caught these two boys stealing my horses. We killed one on my ranch. Rusty and I captured these boys about two miles down the trail. We want to give them to your chief, so he can punish them. Do you understand?"

"Yes, I do."

She spoke softly to the chief in her native tongue.

A smile appeared on the chief's face. He said something to her, and motioned for two braves to come forward and take the Apache boys away.

The girl looked up at the men. "Our chief is very happy you brought these robbers to us. We will take care of them."

The girl looked at Griff. "Mister, my people want to know if you know anything about one of our braves. His uncle, Lone White Feather, sent him out on the desert to have a vision about his future. Did you see him?"

Griff leaned forward in the saddle. "Do you mean Gray Eagle?" "Yes."

Griff could sense she was getting excited.

"He is safe at my ranch. He saved one of my ranch hands, and has become his partner. They go everywhere together."

"Thank you."

"And what is your name?" "White Flower."

"I will tell him I talked to you when I get back to the ranch."

A smile did appear on her face. "Thank you."

Griff and Rusty turned their horses around, and started to head back down the trail. The tribe waved goodbye.

Chapter

6

SUMMER. A week had passed since the amputation of Joe's leg. It was around eight o'clock in the morning. Joe was sitting up in bed looking out the window when Amy came in to see him. Gray was following her with a tray of scrambled eggs and a cup of his special tea.

A serious looking Amy placed the palm of her hand on Joe's forehead.

"How are you feeling this morning?

She removed her hand as she sat down on a bedside chair.

Joe replied, "Just fine. How are both of you?"

Amy was surprised by Joe's upbeat attitude.

"Gray and I are doing fine too."

She studied Joe's eyes.

"I must say it's good to see you getting your health back. All week you have been feverish and dropping in and out of consciousness. That worried me greatly. Usually the patient can get up, and move around a day or two after surgery. I changed the wrapping around your leg twice a day. The leg was healing nicely, so I felt you must have been still suffering the after effects of either the ether or that nasty infection. In your restless sleep you kept mumbling something about landing in a badger hole and having great pain."

"I am fine," Joe replied frankly.

Now, Amy was at ease. "Today, I find you have no fever, and you look alive and alert. They are all good signs. Do you have any pain in your leg?"

"No Madam although it does feel like the bottom part of my leg is still there."

"That is a common feeling. I have talked with a lot of soldiers who have said the same thing. They said it usually went away with time."

Joe gave her a small nod.

Amy touched his right hand. "Sorry, Joe. There is nothing I could do to help your hand. The tendons were too badly bruised."

Joe responded. "Yeah, but I do have little feeling left in that hand."

He held up his right hand. "See! I can move my trigger finger a little."

Both Amy and Gray politely smiled.

Amy continued on. "I did use some liniment to ease the strain I saw in your shoulder. That shoulder should be completely useable."

Joe moved his shoulder a bit and offered a little smile. "It does feel fine. Thanks for all your help."

Amy was a delighted surgeon. She knew she had saved another person's life.

She continued. "Again, I must say this past week has been a tough one. It's been a trying ordeal for all of us here on the Delta D ranch to see you suffer, and almost die. Now, it looks like you will be up and around soon."

"I'm trying. I gotta get out there, and find me a new horse."

Amy smiled again as she started to stand up. "Try not to fall off that horse too?"

Joe knew she was kidding about "Thunder," so he just winked at her.

Amy caught her mistake. She sensed Joe still grieved over the loss of his favorite horse.

"Sorry, Joe."

Gray stepped forward. "I am told this is your favorite breakfast.

The eggs are getting cold. Are you ready to eat?"

"Yes, I am. Hand it over, but forget that damn tea."

Gray placed the tray on Joe's lap, and said, "It's good to see you so alert this morning. I did not hear you during the night. You must have finally slept well."

"Yes, I did because a lot of that damn throbbing in my leg has gone away. I do remember one thing. Whatever Indian tea you have been forcing me to swallow tasted awful, but it must have worked."

"The tea is from the desert willow. I like it."

"I'm glad you like it. Now, would you get me one of Amy's biscuits and a large cup of her black coffee?"

"Sure." Gray nodded, grabbed the cup of tea, and headed to the kitchen.

Amy stood motionless. Joe could see she had something else on her mind.

"Joe, before I had Goldie bury your leg, I asked our blacksmith if he could make a new wooden leg the same size as yours. He measured your leg, and is making you a new one now as I speak, that is, if you want it. He said you could wear it as soon as it is finished. Maybe today."

"You mean like what the pirates wore? A peg leg?"

"Yes, that is exactly what I mean. George is very creative. He has made parts for my buckboard with that old English flair and strength built into them. Coventry was his birth home, by the way, but he says our West is where he wants to be. I know he would make something special for you. What do you say?"

Joe responded, "I like George. He is a quiet chap and a good worker. I don't want to use crutches the rest of my life." Joe paused. "I'm interested. See what he can do."

"Good. That's settled. Enjoy your breakfast."

Amy backed away as Gray came back with two buttered

biscuits and a cup of coffee.

Joe looked at Amy and Gray and thought what better friends could one ever have.

Gray sat down on his cot, and watched Joe eat his breakfast. Joe paid him no mind. He was interested in satisfying the hunger pangs that were coming from his stomach.

Gray waited patiently.

It didn't take Joe long to finish his breakfast. He leaned back against his pillow, and looked at Gray. "What are you staring at? Didn't you ever see a hungry person devour his food before?"

"Yes, a wolf, maybe, but not a man. My people eat very slowly.

They taste their food, not swallow it whole."

A little redness appeared on Joe's face. "You eat the way you want to eat, and I will eat the way I want to eat. Okay?" "Now take my tray away . . . please."

A quiet Gray picked up the tray, and walked out of the room. He felt a little sorry he had upset his leader. White people are much too sensitive, he thought.

"Gray, come back here. I need you."

Gray gave the tray to Amy, and returned to the room. He stood beside Joe's cot. "You need something?"

"Yeah. That coffee is already making me want to crap."

"Mrs. Douglas has a bedpan for you. It's under your cot. I will get it for you."

"I don't want no smelly bedpan, damn it. I want you to help me get off this cot, and go to the outhouse. Remember, it's the one I told you about? All carved pine boards around the seat."

"Yes, I know it quite well. I have used it all week while you were sick," said a stoic Gray.

"Good. Then, help me get off this damn cot."

Joe twisted his body, so he could drop his left foot to the floor. Gray bent down, and placed Joe's right arm under his shoulder. With a careful lift, Gray had him standing up. Joe started teeter tottering on his only leg. Gray held his leader tight. Together, they proceeded to head outdoors, and to the outhouse.

Later, when they reentered the room, someone was standing next to Joe's cot. He had something in his hand "Howdy. I am George Adams, your classic blacksmith by trade."

Joe became a little sarcastic. "I know who you are. It's been quite a while. You made a new scabbard for my rifle. Remember? A bit fancy, I might add."

"I like to put a little style in my work. It makes them last longer. Do you still use it?"

"I did until I had this accident. My right leg is ruined. The scabbard is not much use to me right now. But thanks just the same."

"In India, we have had British soldiers who have lost their right arms, and learned to fire rifles with their left hands. If, by chance, you were ever to use your left hand to shoot a rifle, I could make you a new scabbard, or adapt your old one to the other side of your saddle."

"We'll see?"

Gray helped Joe get settled on the edge of the cot, and then sat beside him.

"What's that strange looking thing you're holding in your hands, George? Is it an English money bag?" a smiling Joe asked.

A bemused, but confidant George offered it to him for his examination "Mrs. Douglas asked me if I could make you a new leg."

Joe held it in his left hand, and marveled. "She told me a short while ago."

He turned the leg around in his left hand observing all the details, and its fine workmanship.

"It's a beauty of design, and it's so light. What kind of wood did you use?"

"A carpenter on the ship coming to America gave it to me. He said he did not like its grain so he gave it to me. I liked its lightness and strength. The carpenter said it was from a tree found in South America. He called it "balsawood." I might add that the leather you see is from a Spanish bull. It is as tough as nails."

Joe was intrigued. "How does this thing work?" Gray moved closer to inspect it.

"It's quite simple. A British surgeon stationed in India told me how he made one for a needy soldier."

George pointed to a leather bag with two leather straps and belt buckles attached to it. The leather bag, he said, was attached to the balsa wood peg leg.

"How does it work?" Joe asked.

George said, "I have put a rolled up piece of cloth in the bottom of the bag to absorb any shock. First, you slide your right leg into the leather bag until it reaches the bottom, and is resting comfortably on the cloth. You tighten each leather strap until you feel the leather bag is snug around your leg. Not too tight. It is not a tourniquet. Then, buckle the straps like you would your pants belt."

"I also added the heel of your old boot to the bottom of the balsa peg leg for safety. You don't want to slip on a wet surface, do you?" George said, with that dry English humor.

"It's a beauty. Polished like the wood of my Winchester rifle. I like it."

"Yes, I used an English stain, and covered it with the sap from a yew tree for extra hardness."

Joe handed it to Gray. "Help me try it on."

George interrupted. "I would suggest you have your Indian friend cut off the bottom half of the jean so it does not bunch up on the inside of the leather bag. In India, everyone wears knickers, so that is not a problem."

Joe agreed and had Gray cut the cloth. Then, he held the peg leg horizontally, allowing Joe to slide his stump into the leather bag.

"Is your stump touching the peg leg?" Gray asked. He was getting better at understanding the white man's lingo.

"Yes, it is. Now, tighten the straps."

After Gray had tightened the straps, and buckled them, he could see Joe was impatient to stand up. Gray grabbed Joe's right shoulder, and gently eased him up off the cot. Joe was a little shaky at first but became more stable as he began to walk. In no time, Joe was walking by himself. Around the cot he went again, and again barely avoiding the chair.

"Thanks for my new peg leg, George. It feels just great. I have two legs again."

George said, "I was told soldiers in India loved them. They could walk ten to twenty miles a day without any problems."

"Good. I will need that help to move cattle and horses around here."

George was finished. He waved a brief goodbye, and went back to his blacksmithing.

"Thanks again!" Joe yelled as George exited the room.

Joe was so excited he walked out of the room, into the kitchen. Amy turned from her dish washing and was stunned by Joe's walking ability.

"Joe, you are doing great. That peg leg looks really good." "Yes, I am very pleased with George's work."

"I told you he was good craftsman."

Joe walked to a chair, and sat down without Gray's assistance. Gray stood behind him for security. Amy stopped drying dishes, and sat down too.

Joe was anxious to know what was happening around the

ranch. "Where are Griff and all the boys?"

"My husband, and the boys as you call them, are returning today after driving a large herd of cattle to rail yards in Bitter Wells. Griff sent Rusty ahead to tell us the good news. The buyers loved our cattle. We made a small fortune on the sale."

"That's good news. Anything else?"

"Yes. The night I operated on your leg, three Apache Indians tried to steal our horses. That was a week ago today. One Indian was shot, and killed, inside the corral. The other two Indians took two of our horses and fled into the night. The next morning, Griff and Rusty followed their tracks all morning to some dusty trail where they found themselves surrounded by big boulders. There, Griff and Rusty captured the two Indians, and turned them over to Gray's tribe for punishment."

Gray was thrilled to hear the news. Nobody had said anything to him till now.

Joe replied, "That's good news isn't it Gray?"

"Yes, it is. My people will take good care of them. Make them work hard."

One more thing that was a bit strange. Griff told me after they carried you in the house; two of our cattle drivers came in, collected the rest of their pay, and said they were finished. They said they wanted to move on, and to see friends up north. Griff thought they were acting rather odd, but he let them go anyway."

"What were their names?" Joe questioned. "Zach Reis and Jonas Dil."

Joe said, "Zach and Jonas are excellent drivers. I'm surprised they would leave like that."

Amy stood up, and offered to get Joe another cup of coffee. He agreed as long as he could have another one of her buttermilk biscuits. She asked if Gray wanted one too.

Amy, Joe and Gray were enjoying their biscuits and coffee, when they heard a commotion coming from the barn. Joe completely forgot his new leg as he stood up, and hobbled out the kitchen door. Gray rose quickly, and walked right behind him.

They could see the barn door was partially open, and they could hear the sounds of a ruckus. Joe peered inside. He saw Curley trying to hold onto the halter of a young, beautiful black stallion. The stallion was shaking its head violently, and fighting the halter. It kicked several times at the wooden stalls, even breaking a board or two.

"What's wrong with the horse, Curley?"

"Hey it's you, Joe. Glad to see you are up and around." At that moment, Curley was reeling so badly, he barely could get any words out. The horse seemed to settle down a little when it saw Joe and Gray.

Curley was enjoying a brief pause. "This horse is one of the two horses Griff bought last week at an auction. He told me to take good care of the horse till he came home. This horse is a brute. Griff said he liked its muscular stature, but he's been in Bitter Wells all week, and hasn't seen its temper. I have, and it's a wild one."

Joe and Gray took a few more steps inside. They could smell alcohol everywhere.

"Curley, you have to be gentle with a young colt like this one. This is a special breed. For one thing, this colt probably doesn't like the smell of whiskey early in the morning. Get what I'm saying to you? You better get somber. Griff is coming home today."

Joe stepped forward, and reached for the halter. Curley relaxed his grip as Joe tightened his left hand around it.

"Joe, he is all yours, and I say good luck." Curley left the barn, and went straight to the bunkhouse.

Joe looked into the colt's eyes. He saw a wildness and freedom staring back at him, but he also saw the loyalty of a true companion. Joe was impressed. He spoke softly to him. "Hi, fellow. I am going to take good care of you. Things are going to get better. I know we'll become good friends."

The colt became quite calm. Joe decided to walk him around the barn, and then he led the colt outside into the corral. Joe studied the colt very carefully. He marveled at its beauty and strength. In Joe's mind, this colt had it all.

Joe pushed a part of mane to the side of its forehead. He saw something that intrigued him. "I see you have a series of white dots coming down your head. You know it reminds me of raindrops. Just like the ones on Thunder's mother."

Joe smiled. "Since rain comes after thunder. "Rain" will be your name."

A stoic Gray standing next to the barn door, had to offer a little grin. He could see his leader was fast on his way to recovery, and the start of a new part of his life.

Chapter

7

AUTUMN. The seasons changed quickly. Autumn came in like a flash. Thundershowers would appear out of nowhere. Big gusty winds would play havoc with the few shade trees on the Delta D ranch. Duke stood on the back porch, and barked often at a leaf or two that were falling in his direction. Amy's flower garden next to the front porch was a wreck with all its colorful petals now polka dotting the lawn. She knew winter was around the corner, so she refused to do anything about it. Griff, always the perfectionist, didn't like it at all, so he made Gray improve the looks of the garden by picking up all the petals and fallen leaves. Gray did not mind it one bit. Griff had made Joe the leader of the few ranch hands that didn't drive cattle, but worked around the ranch. Gray was made Joe's helper. As a bonus, Gray got paid for it. His responsibility was to work with Joe in getting all the chores done around the ranch house, bunkhouse, and barn. Because the cattle drivers spent so much time on the open range, Joe and Gray knew they had a big job on their hands. Deep inside, though, Gray knew his main responsibility was to make sure Joe stayed healthy.

Rain was developing into a fine horse. Although some of the ranch hands offered to bronco bust him, Joe would not allow it. He was determined to train him without breaking his spirit, and, maybe, someday have Gray ride him. Joe wished he could ride him too, but thought better of it. A rider missing a leg and a strained hand, riding on a horse didn't seem like a good idea. Joe did, however, teach Rain to come to him when called.

For quite a long time Joe had to talk to Griff to convince him he wanted to buy the horse. Griff argued with Joe, saying he didn't need a horse. He could use his wife's buckboard to go out on the range, or go to town. Her horse was already trained for the work. Joe persisted, however, and Griff reluctantly agreed to sell Rain to Joe for half a month's salary. It was one of the few times anyone had won an argument with Griff. Everyone knew Griff was as tough as nails when it came to standing by his decisions.

They also knew he was a fair man to work for.

It was a late September day, and the livestock had to be fed. George, the blacksmith, was hurrying trying to roll a wheel he had just repaired. He began to place it onto the axle of a loaded hay wagon. As Joe and Gray were walking out of the barn, they saw George was doubled over, grimacing in some kind of pain. They dropped their tools and rushed to his aid.

"What's wrong George? Need our help?" Joe asked.

"Yeah. My back is killing me. I guess I lifted the wagon wheel the wrong way." George's voice trailed off. He tried to take a deep breath. "Would you help me? My back is killing me. I cannot stand up. I sure would appreciate it."

"Sure, we can do it," Joe replied.

"I just greased the axle," George said.

George shuffled aside as Joe lifted the wheel with his left hand, and mounted it on the axle. Gray handed him the nut, and Joe tightened it with George's wrench. Gray could see Joe had good dexterity using his fingers.

"That looks fine. That nut will last forever. I made it myself." A proud George said as he tried to straighten up once more. He winced in pain.

Joe looked at George, then Gray. He knew what had to be done. He and Gray put their shoulders under George's arms, and carefully supported him across the yard to a cot inside the ranch house. When Amy saw them come in, she dropped her knitting, came into the room, and went straight to the cot where George was lying.

"What's wrong with you, George? She asked.

"My back is killing me."

"Where does it hurt you?"

"In the lower part of my back." He tried to use his hand to show Amy where it was, but it was much too painful.

"I think I know where it is." Amy placed her hand on the center of his back and pressed a little to the right.

"That's it. Right there." At first, George winced, but felt a little relief when Amy removed her hand.

"George, let me tell you at the battle at Gettysburg, some of the soldiers in my troop, tried to lift one of those four-inch cannons, and all suffered a similar back problem. You can bet they didn't try that again. Fortunately, we still won the battle."

She turned, and looked up at Gray.

"There is a jar of liniment on the top shelf in the kitchen, and a towel marked "HOT." Please bring both of them to me."

Gray nodded and hurried to the kitchen.

Moments later, Amy was rubbing the liniment into George's lower back. She massaged the area for a few minutes, and then she placed the HOT towel over the area.

"You stay in that position for ten minutes. Let the liniment do its job. I know it might not be the English way of doing things, but it is my way, and it's the one that had worked best in the United States Army."

George did not move, and stayed in that position for the full ten minutes.

"How do you feel now?" Amy asked. "Much better. Can I lay flat on the cot?"

"Yes, you can but only on your stomach, and stay there for the rest of the day. I will check on you from time to time, and apply more liniment as needed."

"Thank you" said a satisfied and relieved George.

As Amy returned to her knitting, Joe had to ask her a question. "Madam."

"You know better. Stop calling madam. Call me Amy."

"Yes, Amy. I know about your liniment, but what was in that towel? Anyway?"

Amy smiled. "Once Griff had a similar problem like George's. He was carrying a toolbox. He said he tripped walking over some loose rail in the corral. He said he was having a hard time trying to get up. I had to get Rusty and Gus to help him to bed. I was at my wits end trying to figure out what would work better for back pain than just liniment. I thought the liniment was too slow. The following morning, I was on my way to Bitter Wells to see if the doctor could help. As I entered the town, I happened to see an old Mexican woman sitting on a bench. She was applying a cloth to her back. I stopped, and asked her why she did it. She told me she has a lot of back problems, and that the cloth was the only thing that eased her pain. After talking to her, and gaining her confidence, she was willing to show me why the cloth was so good. The woman said she would grind up a variety of Mexican hot peppers and weave them in the threads of the towel. She said they make for a very warm heat and that it was good for her aching bones."

Both Joe and Gray stood speechless. Both were amazed at Amy's abilities to solve everyday problems.

A smiling Amy raised the jar of liniment toward Joe. "Want me to do it to your stump?" she asked.

"No, thanks. I'll wait a little longer."

Before Joe and Gray could reach the kitchen door, Amy spoke. "Joe, how is your new horse doing. Any problems?"

"No problems, everything is going well. You do know I named him "Rain.""

"Yes, I do. You named him Rain because of the white spots on his forehead."

Joe wondered how she knew, but decided not to ask. "Yesterday, I put a saddle on him for the first time. I tightened the cinch, and he didn't move one bit. I'd say in a week or two, I'll have Gray climb into the saddle for the first time. He has been riding one of the other horses, trying to get ready."

"That's good to hear."

Joe could sense Amy had something else on her mind. "Is there something else?"

"No, not really."

With a sudden shake of her head, she turned and walked to the kitchen. She couldn't tell Joe what Elias, the prospector had found under his saddle. Not now, maybe, in the spring. First, she wanted Joe to be healthy, and strong learning to use his new leg.

"Amy, remember Gray and I won't be around here for a while. Griff has his men moving cattle to the lower range, and he wants Gray and me to repair a few fence posts in the south fork. Someone has been cutting the barbed wire. Looks like we might have a rustler or thief on our hands."

"I will keep the supper warm in the oven, if you are not here at dinner time."

"Thanks."

Joe looked at his partner. "Gray, you get the buckboard ready, while I get the rolls of barbed wire, and the tools we will need."

As he headed to the door, Gray saw Joe tug at his peg leg, and grimace a little.

"Is your leg bothering you?"

"I get the feeling of something rubbing my stub. It itches, and it is annoying."

Joe started stomping his peg leg. "Gray, loosen the straps, will you?

He sat down in a chair. "While you're at it, pull the damn thing off." Amy heard some noise, and came back to see what was going on.

"Joe, do you have a problem? Is your leg bothering you?"

"Yeah, it feels like an itch. I have felt it all day. I don't want to be out on the range with this problem."

Amy gently moved Gray aside as she knelt down to take a good look at the stump.

"I see what looks like a rash, but no real swelling around the stump." She peeled some of the bandage away, and carefully checked the end of the stump. "I see nothing there to worry about. There's no blood, or discoloration. I say the end of the stub has been healing well."

Amy stood up, and spoke to Gray. "There is a lotion and some bandages I keep in the cupboard. The lotion is in a gray bottle. Bring both of them here, please."

Gray had seen the bottle and bandages once before and had them back in Amy's hands in no time. She knelt down again, and proceeded to remove the old bandage.

"I am going to rub your whole stub with this lotion, and replace your bandage too. When you put the peg leg back on, make sure you do not tighten the straps too hard.

You need good circulation in that area."

"Okay, I'll walk around on one bare foot, my only foot."

"You do as you are told, unless you want two peg legs. You massage your foot each night."

"Yes, I get the message. Joe said as Amy started the bandaging. Then, she stood up and walked away. Gray replaced the peg leg, and tightened the straps around Joe's stump until they were firm.

Joe stood up, and walking in a circle, tested the leg.

"Gray, the peg leg feels good. Let's get those fence posts done right away. I am getting hungry, just smelling Amy's hot bean soup."

Outside, Gray touched the bag of stones he kept under his arm. Joe didn't notice. It was his way of having self-assurance, that he was following the vision. He raced forward, and opened the barn door first. Gray was anxious to see Rain.

As he reached Rain's stall, he could see something was very wrong. Rain was lying down, and barely moving. Gray yelled in fear as Joe entered the barn. "Rain is down. Rain is down."

Joe moved into the stall, and knelt down beside his horse. He placed his hands on the stomach, and felt all over. He looked up at a very sad Indian boy. "Gray, Rain has some kind of stomach problem. My guess is I think it might be colic. My horse, Thunder had it when he was young. The vet in town said young horses sometimes eat too much sand with the grass. It stops the horse from shitting. The stomach fills up with gas, and the horse loses water."

"Can we do anything for it?"

"We can treat it, and hope that it works. What I did for Thunder worked, but a lot of horses' hearts give out, and they die."

"Get a bucket. Have Amy put a cup of sugar, and a half a cup of mineral oil in it. Then, you fill the bucket with warm water, and stir it. Bring me the bucket, and the bendable tube Amy keeps in the kitchen."

Bendable tube? Gray wondered what's a bendable tube, and why do we need it?

He grabbed the bucket in the corner of the stall, and raced to the kitchen. Amy came out of her knitting room when she heard the door swing open. "What's wrong?"

"Joe wants you to put a cup of sugar in this bucket, and a half cup of mineral oil, and then I am to fill it up with warm water, and stir it." "Why does he want it?"

"Rain is sick. He is lying down in his stall and not moving. Joe thinks it's colic."

Amy dipped a cup into the sugar barrel, and dumping it into the bucket.

"Okay, there's the sugar. Now, you fill the bucket with the water, and bring it to me. I will be in the parlor. I'll get the mineral oil."

Gray carried the bucket outside, and filled it with water from the water box. Then, he hurried inside, to meet Amy who was standing next to a warm fireplace.

Amy dumped the mineral oil in, and stirred.

"Place the handle of the bucket on the hook above the fire. Tell Joe it will be ready soon. There's a good fire under it."

"Yes, madam., I will tell him. He also said he wants the tube that you have."

"It's in the closet next to the ice box," Amy replied. Gray was curious. "What is an ice box?"

"You ask many questions."

"I am sorry, Missus Douglas. I just want to learn about white men." "That's a good thing."

"Griff bought me an ice box last Christmas. It's that wooden box in the corner of the kitchen next to the sink. You open the door, and put ice on the top shelf, and your meats on the bottom shelf. It keeps meat fresh for a few days."

Gray was partly satisfied. He still was having trouble understanding the white man's ways. The people in his tribe let the sun dry out their meat, and it lasts many moons.

He hurried to Joe and told him what Amy had said.

Minutes went by. Joe was getting more concerned about Rain's health. He was afraid, if the water didn't come very soon, Rain would die.

Amy hurries into the stall, carrying the bucket, a little out of breath. "Amy, you should have got one of us to carry the bucket."

"Oh, poppycock. There was no time to lose. I've carried many a bucket to our soldiers. One more won't matter."

She put the bucket in the stall, and handed him the tube.

"Be careful with that tube. It's the only one I have. George made it from some special material he calls rubber. He said he bought it when he was in Brazil. I must say it does work good with all kinds of things."

Joe had Gray lift Rain's head, and he forced the tube down the horse's throat. He looked around for a funnel of some type.

"Amy, get that empty tin can over there. Borrow Gray's knife, and punch a hole in the bottom. Then, bring it over here."

Amy did as instructed.

"Now, Amy, would you place the bottom of the tin can over the end of the tube. Make sure, you keep the hole you just made, right over the center of the tube. I will slowly pour the water from the bucket into the tin can, and let it run down the tube. It should go into Rain's stomach. If, all goes well, once that water gets throughout his body, we should have Rain feeling better."

As Joe was slowly pouring the water, he could see Amy arms were getting tired. "Hold on, just a little longer," he said.

When the task was finished, Joe placed the bucket on the ground, and pulled out the hose. Gray laid the horse's head down on the straw. All three stood, and watched to see if there was any change in Rain's health.

Nothing happened. The horse lay still. Moments passed.

Nothing.

Joe knelt down, and touched Rain's stomach. "I can feel some movement. Something is starting to work." Joe moved his left hand to another part of the stomach. Now, I can even hear some sounds."

They waited.

Then, Rain's eyes opened, and he tried to raise his front legs. All three people were elated as they helped Rain stand up.

At last, a proud Rain was standing tall, though his body still had a little wobble to it. He whinnied to show his approval, while he excreted a large amount of crap.

All three people smiled, and congratulated each other on a job well done. Amy grabbed her tube, and headed back to her kitchen. She was anxious to do her knitting, that is, if no other emergencies arose. But she knew life on the ranch was a twenty-four hour job.

Chapter
8

WINTER. Amy looked out her kitchen window, and stared at a few clouds that were rolling over the mountain peaks. She intuitively knew a bad storm of some kind was on its way. The tree limbs were bare and swaying, the winds were moving in an easterly direction, and a few snowflakes were starting to land on the windowpane. Winter was about to knock at her door, and Amy did not much like it one bit. Last year's winter, she recalled, started with a deluge of large hail balls that pounded all the buildings. Some broke through the barn roof, and killed a pregnant mare. She remembered Griff standing on the porch, fuming, and raising his fist toward what he thought was an evil looking sky. "You sons of bitches, keep your damn ammunition off my ranch. Why don't you try the ranch on the other side of Bitter Wells? They never get the crap you throw at us. See how they like it for achange."

That had been a rare moment. His reddened face and a hacking cough scared Amy. She knew how much Griff loved his ranch, and she did not want to see him get that upset. Somehow, she would try her best not to let that happen again.

Amy looked at the empty water bucket sitting on the dry sink, and realized that she needed clean water. She put her dishwashing aside, and hurried outside.

In the cold, breezy weather, and without a coat, she carried the wooden bucket to a water box. However, when she tried to scoop up some water, she felt the bucket hit a layer of ice. A determined Amy took the bucket, and slammed it down even harder. The ice cracked just a little, so she did it again. This time, the ice broke into pieces, and Amy scooped up a full bucket of icy, cold water.

As she rushed back to the kitchen door, she happened to look up at the windmill. The strong breeze was not moving the vanes at all. Something was wrong. She put the bucket down, and raced to the barn where she knew Joe spent most of his time.

She saw Joe cleaning Rain's stable. "Joe, I need to talk to you."

Joe could see Amy was shivering, and a little out of breath. "Amy, you shouldn't be out here without a coat. It's below freezing."

Amy could see Joe's breath. "The windmill is not working. There is a strong breeze, and the vanes are not moving at all. We need that windmill for all our water needs. Even the animals need it."

"Don't worry I get someone up there to fix it right away. Someone that's in the bunkhouse, maybe, Gus."

"Gus? You're kidding, aren't you? You know he's afraid of heights as well as all the other ones around here. Anything taller than the saddle on a horse scares them, and that windmill is seventy feet tall. You are new to the work around here, I know, but five years ago Griff had to find someone in Bitter Wells who would fix the windmill. His name I seem to recall sounded something like Anderson?"

Gray stopped currying, and stepped out from behind Rain. "Madam, I think you mean 'Man-of-Sun.'"

"Yes, by God, that's it. I remember Griff said he did good work. He climbed up to the top of the windmill, and found some feathers. He surmised a flock of birds must have flown into the windmill, damaging two vanes. Man-of-Sun disconnected the vanes and dropped them to the ground. Griff had George make two new ones out of a stronger metal in his workshop, and Man-of-Sun installed them. We had our water supply again in no time. Griff said the man confided in him that height was no problem for him. He said he was proud to be a half breed, his mother being a member of the Pawnee tribe."

Gray said, "You are right, madam. Like most Indians, Man-of-Sun is not afraid of heights, and he makes a good living doing all kinds of roof repairs. I met him once at the Carlyle School in Pennsylvania where I was being taught English. He helped us to accept the white man's ways, and learn a trade too. He also said he was very sad the old Indian ways were disappearing, so he told us children to learn the new life, but never forget the ancestors and their lives. Needless to say, the school was not too happy with him for saying those things, so they sent him back here."

"Where is he now?" Amy asked.

"He travels around our land. He could be anywhere."

Joe looked amazed.

"That's the most I have ever heard you talk.

Next, you will be giving speeches in town. Maybe run for mayor?" "Joe, don't harass him. He's been a big help around here." Amy responded.

Joe looked at Gray with his eyebrows lowered.

"Amy is right. You are a good fellow and a friend. Go help Amy."

Gray put a blanket around Amy, and walked her back to the kitchen door. He picked up the bucket, and noticed a thin layer of ice was already beginning to cover the surface of the water.

Joe was standing beside the open barn door, watching them go inside. He was sporting a devilish smile." He yelled. "Gray, I want you back here soon. I have a job for you to do."

Both Amy and Gray heard him as they entered the kitchen.

"Don't let him scare you. He is a good man who lost his family a while ago. He was a lonely man for a few years until he found a new home with us."

Amy pointed to the dry sink. Gray placed the bucket on it, and headed back to the barn. He wanted to finish currying Rain, but Joe had other ideas. Joe pointed to the windmill. He handed Gray a pair of tough leather gloves.

At first, Gray refused to take them, but Joe insisted, saying the wooden boards on the frame would tear up his hands. Gray agreed to put them on. Although, he had no idea what to do when he reached the top, Gray did know how to climb, and climb fast. Like a mountain lion going up a tree, he grabbed hold of the first crossbeam on the windmill's frame with his left hand, and then stretched upward with his right hand for the next higher one. In seconds, Gray had reached a platform on which sat a square, wooden box with an open front end. First, Gray gave a quick inspection of the vanes as he inched his way around to the front of the box. The vanes looked in good shape, so he peered into the box, and what he saw amazed him. There was no light toward the back of the box, but in the middle he could see there were two large gears mounted to two axles.

Joe was concerned. "Gray, what do you see? What is the problem?

Gray yelled. "All the vanes looked good, but there is something caught between the gears. It looks black and real ugly."

"What is it, and can you take care of it? We're starting to get more snow, so you have to hurry."

"I am going inside."

Gray crawled inside the box, and pulled out his knife. He poked at the problem several times to see if it was alive. It was frozen solid. Gray did notice it had a reddish head and beak. To his surprise, he realized it was bird, a big bird, like the one he would see flying around the tops of the Uinta Mountains. Yes, he was sure. It was a condor, and there were not one, but two squashed between two large gears. Gray reasoned they were a mating pair that had tried to use the windmill as their nest.

Gray crawled out and yelled down to Joe. "There are two condor birds. Both are frozen and caught between two gears."

"Can you do anything? We need the water."

"I will try again to stab them with my knife. Maybe I can cut off body parts, but it's not going to be easy."

"See what you can do!"

This time, when Gray crawled back inside, he carefully looked the place over. He noticed something in a dark corner of the box. Someone, maybe Man-of-Sun had left a small tool kit. It was quite dusty. It looked like it hadn't been used for quite a while. There was no lock, so he lifted the lid and peered inside. He saw a few rusty tools, but there was one that excited him most: a small sledgehammer.

Suddenly, a strong gust of wind pounded the side of the box with such a mighty force that it rocked the frame. Gray felt streams of air pouring through the gaps in the sideboards as he placed his knife on the dead carcasses and pounded away with the sledgehammer. It was hard work, but pieces of the birds did begin to fall away.

"How's it going?" Joe shouted.

Gray said nothing as he continued chopping at the carcasses. He was getting tired, and each blow had less force. He discarded the gloves, so he could grab the sledgehammer ever tighter.

It was cramped inside the box and Gray could feel the muscles in his arms and legs tightening. He remembered the time he saw two boxers at the school in Pennsylvania. One got so arm weary that he couldn't keep gloves up for protection. The other boxer knocked him out. Gray felt his arms losing power, but he told himself he had to win this battle. He wasn't going to be knocked out.

One final chop, and a big part of one of the carcasses fell away. The gears started turning. The windmill was working again. An exhausted Gray was able to grab both carcasses, and threw them outside. They fell down the side of the frame and landed at Joe's feet.

"What are you trying to do to me? I don't eat condor," a satisfied Joe called.

Gray placed the sledgehammer back in the toolbox and closed the lid. He put his knife back in his belt, and put the gloves back on his hands. He didn't want to hear Joe yell at him about not wearing gloves.

Gray climbed down the frame, and then handed the gloves to Joe.

Joe refused. "Those gloves are the best ones for all the work we do around here. They were mine, but now they are yours. You deserve them."

Gray said nothing.

Joe picked up the carcasses, and threw them in the garbage pitthat was in the far corner of an open field. He knew it would be dinner for the coyotes.

A confident Joe said, "George made that wooden box that's on top of the windmill to stop the snow and ice from freezing on the gears. I guess he didn't figure it would become a nest for condors."

Joe put his arm around Gray's shoulder, and together, they walked back into the barn.

The storm turned into a blizzard. All work on the ranch came to a halt. Some of the ranch hands huddled around a potbelly stove, trying to keep warm. Curley stayed in his bunk offering everyone a sip from a bottle of his least favorite booze. A few tried to play cards, while others wrote letters to their sweethearts, that is, if they had one. Everyone was eager for the snow to stop, so they could make a path from the bunkhouse to the barn and, of course, to the ranch house where they knew Amy was preparing food. Many envisioned they could smell the odors emanating from the kitchen window.

The snow was piling up in big drifts. Moving around outside was nearly impossible. Gray made a pair of snowshoes for Joe. Together, they put on buffalo robes and hats, and decided to trudge to the barn to check on Rain. When they parted the barn doors, they could see Rain moving restlessly. He was nervous. It had never snowed this much before, and it made him skittish. With Joe's guidance, and quiet ways, he was able to walk Rain outside the barn doors, but no further. Rain stood firm in two-foot snow, and then sniffed the air. He whinnied, and looked at both men. Rain became calm, and seemed to understand everything would be all right.

Joe motioned for Gray to walk Rain back to his stall, and to feed him some oats.

Then, Joe reached behind one of the barn doors, and grabbed two large shovels. He handed one to Gray. Together, they attempted to clear a path, but the winds keep swirling the snow around them, and replacing the snow they had just shoveled.

"Gray, we are not making much progress."

Joe had an idea. "Let's make a path through the snow to Amy's kitchen. I know there's a plow that George was fixing. It's in the other end of the barn. You know he is still suffering with a back problem, so why don't we hook up that plow to Rain?"

"How do you hope to do that?" Gray said as snowflakes collected on his cheeks.

"The plow has a pair of straps which we can tie to Rain's saddle. Then, all I have to do is to hold the plow upright while you lead Rain back and forth across the yard. Rain is strong, and with his help, we should make some headway in clearing a path."

Without saying a word, Gray raced into George's work area, and pulled the plow outside. He grabbed the saddle off the rack, and placed it on Rain's back. In no time, the straps were tied to the saddle, and Gray began to lead Rain. In an hour, the yard was cleared of most snow, and the funny thing was, the blizzard died down as well. Both looked at each other with pride for the good work done.

As Gray lead Rain back into the barn, Joe noticed a stranger approaching. He was pushing his way through the snow near the corral, and looked very, very tired.

"What brings you out here in this weather?" asked Joe. "I am looking for Joe Lundy. Is he here?"

"Yes, I am Joe Lundy. What do you want to see me about? It must be pretty important to travel all the way out here?"

"It is!"

Joe could see the man was shivering badly. "Can we step inside the barn for a while. I am damn cold," he said.

"Sure. Gray, bring us a couple of hay bales to sit on, and a blanket." The stranger plopped down, and started his story. "My name is Edward Simpson. I live in Bitter Wells. I work in the telegraph office.

Maybe you have seen me there." "Yeah, I know who you are."

"Well, I have a wife, Betty, and two small children. I also have on my roof a cage I keep for pigeons. If the Indians ever cut the wires, I can send messages to the next telegraph station by attaching a folded piece of paper to the pigeon's leg, and releasing it.

The pigeon, somehow, knows the way to the other telegraph station. We use it only in an emergency situation."

Joe and Gray were interested. "So why would you leave your comfortable home to travel ten miles in this bad weather to see me?" asked Joe.

"Let me explain. I didn't wish to come all this way, but I need your help to find my wife's parents. You see today, I found a new pigeon sitting in my cage. It had a message on its leg, and I didn't know who sent it."

"What did the message say?"

"I read the message twice. It said "STUCK NEED HELP DAD.""

Joe could sense the man was really to pass out. He looked at Gray. "Go get some water. This man needs it."

A minute or two later, Edward was more composed and relaxed.

Joe continued the conversation. "Was the pigeon from another station?"

"No, I checked. So I decided to go to Sheriff Howler for help. He listened to my story, and then said I should see you. He said you are good at solving mysteries, and finding lost trails. So that's why I am here. Can you help me? I don't want anyone to die on my account."

Joe removed his buffalo hat, and scratched his head. "You said the message said 'Stuck, need help, Dad?'" Edward nodded. "Do you know anyone called Dad?"

"I know of no one. My father lives in Missouri, and we all call him pop."

"What about your wife? Does she call anybody dad?

"No, but my six-year-old daughter calls my wife's father, Dada."

"Does your father-in-law have pigeons?"

"Not that I know. I know he likes dogs."

Joe took out his bandana and wiped his brow. "Now, tell me did that new pigeon have snow on its body?"

"Yes, it did. I saw a speck of snow on its head just above its eyes." A puzzled look appeared on Edward's face." What does that mean anyway?"

"Maybe nothing. But I am guessing the pigeon was flying in an eastern direction."

"How far do your pigeons fly?"

"Joe, they can fly hundreds of miles, but ours go only about ten or eleven miles."

"Good. "With the information you have given me, I would say the person or persons who sent that message has a wagon stuck in the Red Cedar Creek about ten miles out of Bitter Wells. Take the Canyon Road west and you will find who sent the message."

"That's great news! Go back to town, and I will ask the sheriff to get a posse right away. I see the sheriff knew what he was talking about when he sent me here."

Ed started to stand up. He was unsteady.

"Hold on a minute. You're in no shape to go back by yourself. Gray and I will take you back in a wagon. We have one with high wheels. We call it our mud wagon."

"Thanks. I would appreciate it." "Please sit down."

"Gray, you get the wagon ready while I tell Griff and Amy what we are about to do. Maybe, I can grab a few of her biscuits for us."

Joe knocked on the kitchen door, and Griff let him in. "It's too early for dinner. What in blazes do you want?"

"We need the mud wagon. Gray and I want to take a stranger named Edward Simpson to Bitter Wells. Sheriff Howler told him to see me. He walked all the way in this damn blizzard. He said he received a message asking for help. I gave him my thoughts on the message, and I want to help him get back home. With Sheriff Howler's help, he believes he will find out who sent the message."

"Okay, do what you do best, but watch that leg of yours. George doesn't have any more of that balsa wood, and we need you here."

"I'll be careful, especially now that the snow has stopped." Gray came into the kitchen with another bucket of water.

Amy looked up from her stew pot and spoke. "That's good thing you are doing, helping Ed Simpson. He has a nice family."

Joe could see Amy looked concern. "Is there anything wrong?" "Well, not really, I guess. Are you using your old saddle on Rain?" "Yes, I am." Now, Joe was concerned. "Why do you ask?"

There was a pause. Amy reasoned whether it was the right time she should tell him what was really on her mind.

"You remember Elias, the prospector, who brought you here on his donkey?

"Yes."

Joe and Gray both wondered what she was going to say next. Amy paused.

Amy reached inside her kitchen drawer and presented a small item to Joe. "Elias said he found it under your saddle and gave it to me. You know what it is, don't you?"

Joe was amazed. "It's a burr. Cockle burr. "What's a cockle burr? Gray questioned.

Griff walked over, and looked at it. He was interested too.

Joe handed it to Gray, and looked at Amy "It is like a thistle with sharp spines. It can make a horse go crazy if it gets into their flesh. But I am surprised. You don't see them around here. Further north, you might. How did it get under my saddle?"

"That is right. You don't see them around here," Amy replied. "Someone must have placed it under your saddle."

Joe took the burr back, and held it up in the light.

"And you believe this is what caused Thunder to act the way he did."

"Yes, I do believe it could have happened that way." Amy looked straight into Joe's eyes. "Who would do that to you? You were on the range when it happened. Could one of the cattle drivers have done it? And why would any of them want to do it?"

"All the drivers are good men. They work hard, and I trust them." "Well, let me say this. You know Zach and Jonas left here in a hurry with their pay when they heard you were alive. They said not a word about how you were doing. They saw us bring you inside. Isn't that just a little strange? Your range partners?"

"I have known Zach and Jonas for a couple of years. They never showed me they would do any underhanded thing like this." Then a thought came forth. "Except, possibly, the last night we were together on the range. We were playing draw poker and I won the pot. Those two men gave me a real ugly look like they thought I was cheating. Zach took out his knife and picked his teeth. He looked uneasy, downright mean. But I tell you I won the pot, fair and square."

Gray stared at Joe.

"You were almost killed," Gray said.

"I think you need to find them, and get this thing cleared up." Griff advised. "Take the mud wagon, and go after them. They need to pay for what they did to you."

"They can't get too far. This winter's been tough. I'll go after them later. Right now, after I get back from Bitter Wells, I must get this ranch in better shape, and that is going to take some time. It's been a hard winter, a lot of the loose boards in the barn need to be replaced first."

Amy started to turn away in disgust. "I did see them talking to Elias right before they rode out. Elias didn't look too happy when he left the next day."

Joe turned, and headed through the kitchen door.

Amy grabbed Gray's arm, and spoke softly. "You watch him all the time, you hear. He is still weak, and he needs to have you nearby. Okay?"

"Yes, I understand. I will do it." Gray hurried outside to catch upwith his leader.

Gray cornered Joe inside the barn. "If you go after those men who almost killed you, you will need some good protection. I saw you have good movement in your left arm hand when you mounted that wagon wheel. Why not try firing some bullets at a few tin cans? I'll set em up on the lower branch of the pine tree in the backyard. You'll need a gun if you go after Zach and Jonas. What do you say?"

Joe was undecided.

He took his hat off and pointed to the gold locket.

"Gray, you see this locket? You asked once what was it? You knew it must be important to me."

Joe opened one half of the locket. "Well, it is a picture of my wife, Abbie."

Joe abruptly closed the locket. "Let me tell you about shooting a gun as you call it. Years ago, I had a small homestead with thirty acres of fertile soil. I had saved my government money that I had made for tracking and killing Indians. Everybody I knew hated the Red Men because of what they did to General Custer and his army unit. I was good with a gun, maybe too good. I had a lovely wife and a baby boy, Joe Jr. We were happy and building a life together.

One day I was coming back from town. I had two mules, one I rode, and the other was loaded with seeds and food items that Abbie wanted. As I approached the gate in the fence, I saw my wife lying against the front door with Joe Jr. in her arms Blood was running down her face. She wasn't moving, and an Indian was kneeling over her, touching the locket that hung around her neck. He didn't see me coming."

"I was so enraged I drew my revolver, and fired four rounds in him. He dropped unto Abbie's lap. I made sure I had saved one round just in case he was still alive."

"I got off my mule, and raced to the door. I overturned the Indian and dropped him on the ground. That's when I could see he was an old man. He was choking on his own blood, but he was still alive."

"Intense hatred was in my eyes and the Indian knew it. I asked him why he killed my wife and child. I had recognized his clothing. He was a Kiowa. I knew some of his language. He could barely speak, but he did tell me that he was on his way to town when he saw a bleeding woman lying next to the door. He said he was trying to feel her heartbeat when I shot him. His last words were he wanted me to tell his sons what happened. I was truly upset and mad. I took my revolver, and threw it as far as I could. I had killed an innocent man who was trying to help my wife and child. I vowed I would never fire my revolver again."

Gray asked, "Did they ever find who killed your family?"

"Yes. The sheriff arrested two drifters, one carried a knife, and they were sentenced to life in a federal prison. They said they did it for food and money, and Abbie fought them. That was a lie. Abbie would never fight them. She would have given them anything they wanted."

Joe paused. He took a deep breath.

"I wanted them bastards hung. I was so bitter."

"And do you have your revolver today?"

"I found it, dusted it off, and threw it in my saddle bag. Now I keep it under my bed wrapped in one of Abbie's bandana. After that, I discovered I could be very effective with my whip at close range and could use my rifle for distance, if necessary."

"That was a while ago. Today, there are few Indians to worry about, but Amy told me there are a lot of rustlers and drunkards and con men roaming these parts. You need your gun for protection." Graypleaded.

"I'll think about it. Let's go see Rain."

Rain stuck his head outside the stable stall and whinnied. He started tapping on the door boards with his right front leg.

Joe reached out and rubbed his hand over Rain's forehead. Gray stood beside his leader. "Good Morning Rain. Are you ready for your saddle and a rider this time?"

Rain agreed with another whinny. "Good."

"I see there's little snow left. Gray, get the saddle and blanket off the table, and let's saddle him up. I am hoping Rain will let you on his back. Are you ready?

"Yes, I am ready."

Minutes later, Joe was walking Rain out into the corral. Curley and Goldie were mending a portion of an old fence. Both looked up to see Joe hold Rain steady while Gray approached Rain's side. Joe gave a few pats on Rain's neck for reassurance as Gray placed his left foot in the stirrup, and began to slowly climb aboard. Rain shifted the increased weight on his front legs, but showed no signs of resistance. Rain's eyes were steadfast on Joe's. It was a trust that only a man and his horse can know.

Joe released his grip on the halter, and stepped aside. Rain stood patiently waiting for the next command. Gray shook the reins slightly, and put his heels in Rain's side.

"Let's go, Rain." urged Gray as pressed his heels against the horse's sides.

Rain began to walk, and Gray steered him outside and around the inside of the corral. Several times Gray would do this occasionally stopping and starting. A rider relationship between both of them was developing.

Joe watched with keen interest. "Gray, make sure you do just the things I have taught you."

Gray nodded.

"I think that is enough for today. Bring him back into the barn."

Gray stopped the horse at the barn door and dismounted. He

removed the saddle as Joe took hold of the halter and led Rain into the stall. Joe patted Rain's neck and began to curry his soft black hair. "Today you did well, my friend, real well. Tomorrow, Gray will ride you some more, and by the end of the week, he should be able to take you for a ride on the open range."

Rain turned his head, and looked at Joe. It was eye-to-eye contact again. No sounds were made, but Joe knew somehow Rain wanted him on his back.

"Maybe someday Rain. Maybe."

Gray stepped into the stall, and patted Rain's hindquarters.

Joe looked at Gray. "Good riding. Be ready tomorrow for more."

Gray picked up another currycomb and began to help. He was quite pleased.

As Joe leaned over to pick up a bucket of water, Gray saw the gold locket on Joe's hat come loose and fall. In an instant Gray grabbed the locket in midair. Joe looked surprised when Gray handed it back to him. No words were spoken.

Two more weeks went by. Unbeknown to Joe, George had been asked by Amy to see if he could create a special stirrup for Joe's false leg to fit into. Without Joe knowing, George spent his evenings measuring Joe's saddle and right stirrup. In a short time he had fashioned a new stirrup and, secretly, he attached it to the saddle. Gray was made aware of the ruse.

Morning came, Joe and Gray walk into the barn. Joe held Rain by the halter while Gray placed a blanket over Rain's back. He picked up the saddle, and heaved it over the horse's back. He got everything aligned, and began to tighten the clinch.

Joe sensed there is something that was not right. He looked around Rain's other side, and saw the new stirrup. "What's this for? Who did this?" Joe was perplexed and a little angry.

Gray tried to ease Joe's anxiety. "Amy wants you to get back on a horse. She thinks you are not sure of yourself since that accident you had with Thunder. She wants you to get over your fear."

"She does, does she? She is not my wife or my boss. You tell her I said so, and to keep her nose out of my business."

"Why don't you tell me, big man?" It was Amy standing inside the barn door.

A surprised Joe stared at Rain, then Amy. He was embarrassed.

He respected Amy.

"Okay, Joe. You don't always like what I do, but this time I believe I am right. I had George make a new stirrup so you could climb aboard, swing the top part of your right leg over the saddle, and place the false part into a stirrup made especially for you."

"Why now? There is still much work to be done around here."

"I know that, and Griff knows it too. We both agree you are the type that needs to be riding the range, at least once in a while."

Joe looked at Gray. "Did you know about this?"

"He did not," said Amy. "Only Griff, George and I knew about it. So get Rain outside, and let him know who is boss."

Amy turned and headed back to the ranch house.

Joe looked at Rain, and stared into his eyes. "I guess it's about time for you and me to make some trails together." Rain gave a soft whinny.

Once outside, Joe placed his left boot into the stirrup, and swung his peg leg over the saddle, and into the new stirrup. He gently pulled on the reins, and steered Rain out of the barn into the bright sunlight. Together, they headed toward a snowy hill and disappeared into the morning mist.

Gray was so pleased that even he cracked a big smile, but no one ever saw it.

Chapter
9

Bang!

The forty-five-caliber bullet whizzed past its intended target, a large tin can, and buried itself into the trunk of an old pine tree.

"What's wrong, Joe? You missed the tin can. That should have been an easy one. It's only fifteen yards away." Gray was annoyed, but he would not let his face show it.

Joe countered. "Look around you. What do you see? A light snow is falling everywhere. A breeze carried a snowflake into my left eye. I blinked. That's all."

Gray gave no response, but carried a smaller tin can to the tree, and set it on the branch partially behind the larger tin can. Then, he walked back to where Joe was standing.

"I will count to three once again. You draw, and try to hit the second can."

Gray noticed Joe appeared less nervous this time. He had stopped flexing the fingers on his left hand. It was a sure sign Joe was getting more relaxed.

"You can do it."

"I don't need a pep talk. Start counting." Joe took his position; both hands were hanging down, waist level.

"One. Two. Three."

Joe's left hand pulled the revolver out of its holster in one fluid motion. It was a very fast, a blinding draw. He fired the revolver, and the bullet tore a large hole down the side of the second tin can, and it fell to the ground. The large tin can still sat on the tree branch, untouched.

Griff was watching a distance away, and clapped. "Great shooting. What's next?"

Joe and Gray turned to see their boss standing outside the

kitchen door. He was holding a silver dollar, and like a magician was twirling it around his fingers. "Let's see how good you really are. Joe, I am going to flip this silver dollar into the air. I challenge you to put a bullet hole through it. If you do, you can keep the dollar. Are you up for it?"

"Flip your dollar high in the air!"

Griff stepped away from the door. Using his strong fingers, he flipped the dollar at least, twenty feet in the air, rotating it end over end. Once again, with one fluid motion, Joe drew his revolver and fired. The silver dollar immediately stopped rotating, and dropped to the ground. Griff picked it up out of the snow, and stared at it. A perfect hole was through its center.

Griff gave the coin to Joe.

"Well, I am amazed. You shoot better with your left hand than you ever did with your right. Remember, we tried this trick a few years ago. You used your right hand then, and could only nick the edge of this dollar."

Griff smiled. He opened the palm on his other hand. "See there. That's the nick. This is that same dollar. I have saved it all these years as a souvenir. Now it's yours." Griff flipped both silver dollars to Joe. "Great shooting this time."

As Griff went back into the house, Gray had to ask. "That was great shooting, but he said you could not hit the dollar with your right hand?" Joe smiled. "I knew I could've put a hole through this coin with my right hand, but I didn't want our boss to think I was a gunslinger. I am a cowboy, first, who knows how to use his weapons." Joe held up the souvenir coin. "I nicked this one just to make my mark. I didn't want

Griff to know the truth. And don't you tell him."

Gray said nothing, but was intrigued by the white man's ways of doing things.

A somber Joe said, "Let's get out of this weather, and go to the bunkhouse. I want to show you something I have always carried with me. It saved my life a few times during the Indian wars that we had over in the next county."

As Joe and Gray walked away, a sudden blast of cold air hit them head on. "This is supposed to be spring, and we are still suffering the woes of winter." He growled.

Gray pulled a small bag from under his arm. He opened it, and let three colored stones roll out onto the palm of his hand. "What's that? Are you a weather forecaster now?"

A very soft smile appeared on Gray's face. "No, but these stones tells me what awaits both of us. They are my good luck charms as a white man might say."

Gray pointed to a round blue stone. "This one came out first. It is the color of the sky. That means winter is over, and warm weather is coming real soon, maybe tomorrow."

"Sure. What else does it tell you? Where the gold is in these mountains around us?"

Gray ignored the question, and looked at the second stone. It was brown, and not very round, but it did have a pointed end. He showed Joe the stone. "This stone was pointing in the direction of Bitter Wells. Something is going to happen there in a month, and it's going be good for you."

"How do you know it's a month, not a year?" "See that dark wavy line on top of the stone?" "Yes, I see it. So what."

"When that is showing, it means a month." Gray could see Joe was disgruntled.

"And what does the third and final stone tell you?"

Gray stared at the jagged piece of black onyx. He didn't want Joe to know what it said.

"Well, what does it say?" Joe was abrupt because he felt the effect of the cold air creeping into his bones.

"It tells me you are going to meet a bad man who shoots as good as you." Gray could not bear to tell his leader what the rest of the stone was telling him.

"A bad man? A gunslinger? I've met a lot of them in my life. Each one falls by the wayside. No one is the fastest gun out here for long."

"It might not be a fast gun." Gray offered.

As Joe opened the door to the bunkhouse, he said, "Put those things back in your bag, and hide them under your arm. I don't want anyone to know you have them. We'd be laughed out of Dodge City. And besides, I like my warm bed."

They entered the bunkhouse, and could see nobody was there except Curley who was lying in bed with his hand wrapped around a bottle. Joe paid no attention to him as he walked over to a buffalo horn hanging on the wall above his bed. He grabbed something that looked like a coiled up rattlesnake off of it.

"This is a whip. It is the best thing for close fighting with your enemy, that is, if you know how to use it."

Joe held the handle, and let the whip uncurl itself.

"The motion of the whip and the strike, as I call it, are all in your wrist. See that bottle Curley is holding? I could take it out of his hands in an instant when I could use my right hand." Joe's voice went silent for a moment. "Instead of counting coup (touching the enemy with a stick) as the Indians do, I counted the lives of the warriors that I saved. Indians that were just damn drunk, not bad criminals."

Joe handed the whip to Gray. "You'll the feel of the leathergrip."

Gray squeezed the soft leather and waved the whip. It was a haphazard attempt, and almost broke someone's ceramic spittoon.

"Easy there. It takes some time to learn how to use the whip. But once you learn you never forget it. When that spring weather does come, I'll try to show you the secrets of good whipping."

Gray answered. "I cannot wait. And I will show you how I use my knife."

"You've got a deal."

Gray pointed to the buffalo horn. "I always wanted to go on a buffalo hunt. My uncle told me many tales how the Nuchu, crawling on their arms and knees, would sneak up on a herd, pick out the biggest one, and shoot one arrow. If it were a perfect hit to the heart, they would wait until the animal dropped over. Then, they call the women who would hurry out with their knives. They would skin the animal, cut the animal up into pieces, and take it back to camp."

"Didn't they have horses like the other Plains Indians?"

"No, the buffalo was a sacred animal. It deserved the right to live where it wanted to. The Nuchu would honor the ways of their hunting ancestors."

Rusty, Goldie, and Gus barged through the ranch house door. They began to dust the snowflakes off their fur coats. All of them had dour looks on their faces. Joe thought it was unusual for Goldie. He was usually the jokester in the group.

Joe wondered what was wrong. "Hey, boys! What are you so sad about? I know the weather is still bad, but the cows out on the range can handle it. I bet the temperature doesn't go below freezingtonight."

No one cared to answer his question. That's when Joe really knew something was wrong.

"Okay. Let me in on the secret. Who lost his money playing poker?" A startled Rusty felt he had to answer back.

"Yeah, we were in town, and we did lose a few dollars, but that's not the problem."

"What is it then?"

Rusty hesitated to answer, and looked around the room. Joe could see he was unhappy.

"It's this way, Joe. We left the cows in the north fork. They were grazing peacefully on the hay we had brought them. Things were easy. No problems. Bitter Wells, you know, is not that far away, so we decided to do a little gambling in Dave's Saloon. Mind you, it was for only four hours at the most. Well, when we returned to check on the cows, we could see a half a dozen or more were missing. Goldie spotted blood on the snow, and we followed the trail. It led to a bad scene. Those cows had been slaughtered and were laying in a circle of blood."

"What do you think happened?"

Gus spoke up. "It looked like someone was leaving us a message."

Rusty continued on. "Somebody with the skill of a surgeon or a butcher cut the choicest parts of meat right out of the cow. The cuts were clean and sharp. Whoever did it knew what they were doing, I can tell you that."

Joe questioned. "But why would they do that instead of rustling them off our range?"

Rusty took off his Stetson hat, and shook his head. "I don't know. I do know we lost a few hundred pounds of good meat, and this weather will keep it from going rotten for quite a while if the wolves don't get to it first."

"Did you see any hoof prints? Any trail they might have left?" Joe asked.

"Goldie thought he saw the marks of a wagon wheel in the snow about a hundred yards away." Rusty stopped talking. "I hate to tell the boss."

Joe could see Rusty was quite upset.

"Don't worry about it. I will tell the boss myself."

A fearful Joe had to ask. "I hope you moved the rest of the herd to another place?"

"Yes, we did. We moved them to the south pasture." "You did the right thing."

Joe looked out the window. "It's getting late, and the snow would have covered any tracks by now. We would never find who did it. Griff will probably go to town tomorrow if it stops snowing, and talk to the sheriff.”

Joe was concerned. How was he going to keep Griff from losing his temper?

Clang. Clang. Clang.

Amy Douglas was on the porch ringing a metal triangle. It was dinnertime.

“There you go. It is our dinnertime. We don’t want to spoil Amy’s good cooking, do we? I will wait till after dinner to tell Griff. He iseasier to handle when he has a belly full.”

“Let’s eat!”

Chapter
10

Griff Douglas towered over the sheriff, who was sitting behind his desk, rolling a cigarette. Griff had the stern look of a Boston Bulldog. The tone of his voice was to pressure the sheriff into immediate assistance. His foreman, Rusty, who remained silent, stood a step behind him.

"Tom, someone butchered about ten of my cows out on the range late yesterday afternoon. Those bastards cut out only the choicest cuts of meat and took off. We couldn't trail them because of the weather. I believe whoever did it might have come into your town."

Tom Howler had been the sheriff in Bitter Wells for five years. He was a tall fellow, rather slender, with bushy eyebrows and a handlebar mustache. He had the ability to handle all situations that might come his way. Drunks and young dudes who came into his town for a little fun were no problem. Tom had the tact and know-how to settle all their disagreements. Everyone in town thought well of him. As a reminder that he meant business, he liked to keep his cavalry revolver on the desk. Anyone who entered his office and tried to reach for it would be hogtied and thrown into jail, no questions asked. He was the power who wanted the people to know that Bitter Wells would always be a safe place to live.

Tom took a wooden match out of the desk drawer and flicked it across the bottom of his shoe. The match caught fire, and he proceeded to light his cigarette. He took a short puff and threw the hot match into a spittoon that was by his left boot.

"Griff, slow down a bit, will you?" Tom retorted. "This is the first time I have heard about this. I know you haven't been in town for quite a while. How is Amy doing these days? Still knitting, I take it."

"Stop with all the knitting crap. Amy is fine. I have a problem, and I need your help."

"Sure. You have it. Anytime."

"Good. Let's get down to business. My ranch hand, Goldie, thought he saw a wagon rut in the snow."

Tom stared up at Griff. "Did you see it?" "No, I did not."

Tom was a little confused. "How did Goldie see it, but not you?" "It was dark when I got to the spot where this happened."

"My men thought the cattle were safe being alone in the south fork, so they came into town to play a little poker. When they returned to the range, they saw the ten steers lying in a bloody circle. That is when Goldie claimed to have seen the wagon wheel rut."

"So if I get this straight, no one was minding the fort. The thieves rode in, killed the steers, placed them in a circle, and took what meat they wanted. Is that correct?

"Yes, it is. I know my men made a mistake, a big one, and they will pay for it. I guarantee you that. But first, I want to get those bastards who killed my cattle. I don't want this to ever happen again."

"Okay, I get it. What do you want me to do?"

"Find out if a wagon came through here late yesterday."

"That's a tall order, don't you think?" Tom responded. "We have a lot of farmers and ranchers who come into town every day. Each one brings a wagon carrying all kinds of grain and produce."

Griff nodded. "I understand that, but will you check around and see if anything suspicious happened late yesterday afternoon."

"I'll do better than that. I have Jessip, our town gossiper, come in. He knows more about what goes on in this town than I do."

Griff looked puzzled. "I never heard of a Jessip. Who the hell is he?"

Tom smiled. "Jessip came walking into Bitter Wells a year ago. He had no money, and nobody knew where he came from. The livery stable owner gave him a temporary job cleaning out the stables and grooming the horses. The owner was forced to let him go when things got tight. So Jessip told a tale about his life to the local newspaper, and began scooping for them ever since. I mean getting good news stories to print."

"When can I meet him?"

"Right now, I suppose. He probably saw you come in here. My guess he is sitting outside my door trying to hear what we are talking about. If he likes what he hears, he goes to the newspaper office and tells them. They, in turn, give him a few silver coins. That's how he makes his living today. He has also become my second pair of eyes and a good friend to boot."

Griff looked over his shoulder. "Rusty, go open the damn door."

Rusty turned the knob and yanked the door wide open. Sure enough, a short, scrawny man with large eyes and a big nose was trying to sit back down in the chair.

"The sheriff wants to see you." Rusty announced.

Jessip slowly rose from his chair and entered the office. He acted like a child afraid of what his father might do to him. Cautiously, he stepped up to the sheriff's desk with a bowed head.

"Jessip, these men are from the Delta D ranch about ten miles out of town." Tom pointed to both of them while taking another puff on his cigarette. "This is Griff Douglas. He owns the ranch along with his wife, Amy. And the other fellow with the checkered bandana is Rusty, his foreman."

A shy Jessip looked up at the men and nodded a little. Griff and Rusty nodded back.

"Jessip, Griff had ten cows butchered on his ranch. They were not rustled, just simply butchered on the spot, and somebody took several choice cuts of meat. Griff thinks the ones who did this thing had a wagon and came into our town late yesterday afternoon. I know you keep an eye on everything going on in this town, and I appreciate your help."

"Did you see anything unusual yesterday afternoon?" Tom

asked. Jessip thought for a moment. "Sheriff, everything was about the same except I did see something a little strange late in the day."

"What was it?" Griff interjected."

The shy Jessip kept looking at Tom. He looked like he was afraid of something.

"What was it, Jessip?" The sheriff insisted.

"It was about seven o'clock at night. Two men were driving a wagon. It had a very heavy load. I know because the rear wheels sank deep into the ground. They came into the back of town, and hid the wagon behind Grannies General Store. I watched from back of the saloon as they unloaded several burlap packages, and carried them inside her store. I am sure she paid them, and they left in a hurry. One of them looked back in my direction. He grinned, and I didn't like it."

"Did you see who the men were?" Tom asked. "Yes, but I am afraid if I tell you, they will kill me." "Why do you think that way?"

"Early today that little man with a butcher knife in his hand saw me in Dave's Saloon, and said to me the one thing he hates more than an Indian is a snooping rat. He was looking straight at me when he said that."

Tom was moved. "Jessip. I will protect you. Okay?" "Now who is it?"

Jessip seemed a bit unsure. He stammered a bit, but decided to tell his story.

"I saw the two men gambling in Dave's Saloon the night before. I believe they lost all their money to that fancy dressed gambler who came in on the stage two days ago. The small man liked to take his sharp knife out of its sheath, and pick his teeth. He said beef gets caught between his teeth. The other one had a scar above his left eye. I notice things like that. It makes for good news. The editor says I do real good."

"Thanks, Jessip. You did well. Wait outside while I finish with these two men.”

“Sure, Tom. Now, don’t forget you said you are going to protect me.”

“I won’t forget.”

Griff and Rusty looked at each other. Both knew who those two men were.

“Sheriff, those two men were working for me until a month ago. Their names are Zach Reis and Jonas Diver. They’re good cattle drivers, but it looks like they were bad losers at the card table.”

Jessip couldn’t wait. He hurried out of the office, and scampered straight across the muddy street to the newspaper office.

Tom had a thought. He opened the desk drawer once again, and pulled out a handful of papers and posters.

“Zach Reis. I seem to remember that name.”

Putting the papers aside, he sifted through the wanted posters until he found the one he was looking for. He showed it to Griff and Rusty. “Is this the man you are looking for?”

Griff answered. “Yes, that’s the one. Like I said he worked for me until a month ago.”

“That man broke out of jail in Orem County three years ago. He has been on the run ever since. We just cannot seem to catch him.” Tom said.

“What did he do?” Griff wanted to know.

“He was found guilty of killing the butcher in Jackrabbit Flats with the butcher’s own knife.

“Where do we find him?” an anxious Griff asked. “He’s on the run. He could be anywhere.”

“What about the other guy, Jonas Diver?”

Tom searched through the wanted posters again. “There’s nothing here. He is clean. Zach must have met up with him somewhere along the way.”

Griff and Rusty stepped back. They were ready to leave.

With two fingers, Tom snuffed out the burning end of the cigarette and laid it in an ashtray. It would be ready for future use. He got up from his desk in a hurry, and grabbed his revolver. "Let's get those men before they leave town. If they had any money left, they would be spending it in the saloon."

Tom pushed the saloon doors open. A man who was exiting, decided it was better to step aside. The place was half filled with grizzled old men sitting at tables, guzzling local beer, and smoking terrible smelling cigars.

Tom walked over to a table where a white bearded heavy-set old codger was playing a card game called Mexican Sweats. The man paid no attention to them. He stared at the cards in his hand.

"Snake, I'd like to talk to you."

The man continued to stare at his cards. "Snake, I said I would like to talk to you!"

The three other men sitting at the table started to get up to leave. "Sit down, all of you. I have a question for the Snake. That's all."

Tom laid his polished revolver down on the table next to the Snake's hands.

The Snake did not look up but spoke words that seem to slip out the side of his mouth. "You know I don't like you, and I don't rat on my friends."

"Forget the bullshit. I want to know who lost all their money yesterday. That's all."

The old codger got the message.

Without looking up, he said, "See the gambler with the pretty suit sitting over in the corner counting his money? He's not my friend, and he is the bastard that came in on the stage two days ago. Yesterday, he took two men for all they had. The Good Book always says to leave a little behind for others. That bastard leaves nothing."

"Did one of them have a fancy knife?" Griff asked. The Snake did not answer.

"Okay. That's all I need from you today. Maybe next time you will be more friendly when I have more of my friends with me." Tom picked up his revolver.

Snake yelled "I have a dead man's hand!" and pulled all the money off the table. He could care less about anything else.

The gambler looked up at the three men who were coming toward his small table. He was clean-shaven with a pleasant smile. His grooming was immaculate. He put his wallet back inside his vest pocket and pulled out a slim gold case. He took a European cigarette out of it and lit it with a gold-tipped match. He proceeded to take a long, slow draw on it just as the three men reached his table.

"What can I do for you, Sheriff?"

"I would like to know who you were gambling with late yesterday.

One of them might be carrying a butcher's knife?"

"I gamble with a lot of people. I could care less about any of them. It's their money I'm after."

"Well, you better care, or you'll be sitting your ass in a jail cell. Do I make myself clear?"

"On what charge?"

"You pick one. Any one will do."

The gambler tipped the front edge of his Stetson hat upward.

Everyone could see a fresh five-inch gash that ran across his forehead. "This is what I have to show for playing poker with that jackass. I tell you that man with the knife is plum loco."

Tom wanted more. "What happened?"

"After the last hand was over, he jumped on the table, and slashed my forehead with that knife of his for no good reason. I think he has a problem with any other person winning. That guy goes loco. He said he wanted to keep his knife, even though I won it fair and square. I hate to lose money, but I am not a fool either. His partner had his gun pointed at me. I'm a peaceable man, most times, so I gave him half of the money he lost, and said he could keep the knife. I didn't like the damn thing anyway."

Tom replied, "You should have got me. I would've thrown his ass in jail. He's on my wanted poster list. You would have got a reward."

"How much reward?" "One hundred dollars."

"Do you pay it, if I bring him dead or alive?" "It's your choice."

Griff spoke next. "Do you know where he is now?"

"I understand he and his partner were leaving town in a hurry." "Do you know where they went?" Tom pressed him for a name.

"They were talking about heading north, maybe, to Miner's Creek or even up to Deadwood. They had some friends up there. I know I would hate to be one of those poor fools. You don't know when he will go loco."

"Okay. That will do."

"By the way, what's your name, and how long will you be in Bitter Wells?"

"My name is Dallas Grat. I usually go to each town where Elmar's Snake Oil wagon will be. He should be here by tomorrow morning."

Griff had to ask. "What is this snake oil wagon you are talking about, and why is it coming to Bitter Wells?"

Dallas was getting tired of answering questions. He stood up, all six and a half feet of him, and started toward the bar. "I'll see you all later. I need another drink."

Tom turned to Griff and Rusty. "That snake oil wagon he just mentioned must be the same one that Jessip saw when I sent him on an errand to another town last week. Now I know, for sure, it's coming to our town next. There will be some pretty women to see sing and dance, and games for everyone. Should be a good time as long as nobody drinks too much."

Tom pointed to the saloon doors. "Let's make one more stop at Grannie's General Store. That's where those men parked their wagon. Maybe she knows what is going on."

Griff nodded, and the three walked out of the saloon. He followed the wooden sidewalks that led to a large square building painted dull red.

Three ladies in their fancy dresses and feathered hats were looking at new clothes. One of them saw Rusty and gave him a sexy wink. It was Molly. She was looking at new white bloomers. Rusty smiled, and tipped his hat as if to say I'll see you later.

Tom and Griff walked up to the counter. A friendly older lady, with her grayish hair tied up in a bun, greeted them. "Hello sheriff, I see the warm spring weather is finally here, and what brings you to my store? Do you need any supplies? I have a sale on leather belts."

Tom smiled, but he wasn't interested in belts. "Grannie, you know Griff from the Delta D ranch?"

"Well, I know of him, but I never really met him until now. "Hello Griff. It's nice to meet you."

Griff responded. "Hello to you Madam. It's my pleasure to meet you. I have to apologize for not meeting you sooner. I am so busy on the ranch that I have little time for anything else. I always send one of my workers into town for whatever supplies we need."

Tom spoke. "Grannie, Last night someone was seen riding a wagon up to your back door, and unloading items wrapped in burlap. Do you know who he was?"

"Sheriff Tom Howler. Do you suspect me of doing something bad?" "No Grannie, but someone butchered ten cows on Griff's ranch yesterday. We think they came into our town. What was being unloaded last night behind your store?"

A frown appeared on Grannie's forehead.

"Well, all right, if you must know. I was trying to keep it a secret, but now when I tell you that snoopy little man of yours will find out, and tell the newspaper editor. Then, the surprise will be lost."

"What is the surprise?" Tom had raised his voice a little.

"Well, don't get huffy. I don't want the ladies in here to know what I am telling you, so I am going to talk in a lower voice. Two men came into my store yesterday afternoon, and said they had lost all their money playing poker in Dave's Saloon. The shorter one said he lost his favorite knife to some big time gambler. He wanted it back, but needed two hundred dollars to buy it back. He said he had found out what my surprise was going to be, and knew I needed a lot of beef to make it happen. Since my regular supplier hadn't come, I agreed, and gave him my old hunting knife. He promised to have the beef to me later that night. They delivered it on time, and I gave him the two hundred dollars. They drove off in their wagon, and that's the last time I saw them."

"That man lied to you. He got his knife back before he saw you." "You gave them two hundred dollars for stolen beef?" Griff was outraged.

Tom touched Griff's shoulder to calm him down a bit. He asked Grannie. "Didn't you think something was not right? Where were they going to get all that beef?"

"The man conned me. He said he worked on a ranch, and they owed him a few cows. He seemed like he was telling me the truth."

Tom said with firmness in his voice. "Well, Grannie, You have two choices as I see it. You can give all the beef back to Griff, or you can pay him for it."

"I can't pay another two hundred dollars. I'll be out of business."

A calmer Griff could see a real sadness come into her face. She was a hardworking and honest citizen caught in a scam. "Grannie, may I ask what the beef was for?"

"Tomorrow will be Doc Markis's fiftieth birthday, and I wanted to have a little party for him and his family. He saved several townspeople who were deathly sick last year. That's all."

"Yes, Grannie, two of my men were on their death beds and the doc saved them." Griff paused. "You keep the beef as my way of helping you with the party. All I want to do is catch those men and put them in jail."

Tom was pleased to add. "Grannie, there is a wagon coming in tomorrow. It is called Elmar's Snake Oil Wagon. It's supposed to have games for the men and the children. That should go well with your party."

As all three men started to walk back to the sheriff's office. Rusty mentioned, "Did you notice Zach never told her about the gash he did to Grat's forehead, or the money he got back."

Tom said, "If those two men are in the next county, they are out of my jurisdiction. I can do nothing about it."

Griff was still upset. "What do you mean there is nothing you can do?"

"I'll notify the officials in the surrounding counties and towns.

Someone will catch those men."

"That's it. Maybe that's all you can do, Tom?"

Tom nodded as he opened the office door, and went inside.

Griff and Rusty climbed aboard Amy's buckboard and started out of town. Griff was very disappointed, but had some ideas he wanted to discuss with Joe when he got home.

Chapter
11

SPRING. The sun's rays were melting the remaining traces of snow and ice as Joe and Gray rode into Bitter Wells. Main Street was turning into a muddy mess. Farmers with their wagons were coming into town to pick up needed supplies, their wheels gouging out blobs of mud that flew in all directions. Ladies in their nice outfits stayed close to the buildings as they walked along the wooden sidewalks. Everyone seemed to be waking up from a long winter's nap.

"I guess bears aren't the only ones that hibernate." A smiling Joe said as he surveyed the activities.

"Watch out, Joe." Gray warned.

A little man with a big nose, carrying a piece of paper, kept hopping from one mud hole to another, until his feet landed him in front of Rain's nose. Rain whinnied his displeasure as Joe pulled back on the reins. Not saying a word the man kept moving forward until he reached the other side of the street, and then disappeared into the newspaper office.

"Who the hell was that? I could have run over him!" Gray offered no reply.

Joe and Gray steered their horses over to the hitching post in front of the sheriff's office. Down the street, they could see the ground next to Grannie's General Store was covered with straw. The townsfolk were gathering around a giant teepee that was sitting on top of a Conestoga wagon, something Joe thought he might have seen at one of Buffalo Bill's Wild West Shows. All kinds of writing and colorful pictures painted on its sides.

"Looks like they're having a shindig of some type. We'll check it out later. First, I want to see the sheriff," Joe said as he dismounted.

Inside the office sat the sheriff who was listening to the rather chubby old mayor complaining about what was happening to his town. The mayor seemed upset, but stopped the conversation when he saw Joe and Gray enter. With a tip of his bowler, he excused himself, and hurried out the door.

"Hi, Tom. What's that all about? The mayor looked annoyed at something."

"Oh, it's nothing really. The mayor is always in a nervous mood. He is afraid we don't have enough deputies to handle the crowd that is down the street. They're getting anxious, waiting for the show to begin."

"What kind of show is it?"

Tom sat back in his chair, and lit up a homemade cigarette. "Some guy named Elmar Root travels from town to town, and sometimes he stops here. He puts on a little show with young female entertainers. The women working at Dave's Saloon don't like it much. They would argue and it was hurting their business."

Tom leaned forward and frowned. "And don't get any ideas, Joe. These girls are too young for you."

Tom relaxed back in his chair as Joe asked, "Is Elmar's show hurting the other businesses in this town?"

"No, not at all. The farmers and the ranchers bring their entire families. Elmar opens the back of his wagon, and makes it into a stage. He lets the women sing and dance to the music of an old fiddle player, and then he tries to sell some kind of snake oil. He claims it cures everything, even drunkenness. The bartender already has bought ten bottles of that stuff. I can tell Elmar is a real showman. I hope he is not a crook."

"What about the last time he was here? Did you arrest him?"

"No, I did not!" Tom opened the bottom drawer and held up an empty bottle. "I bought one of these for four bits. He said it cured dysentery, and it did. It tasted like blackberry wine. Real good stuff."

"So what makes you think he might be a crook?"

"Nothing really, but last time he was here an elderly woman claimed she lost her diamond necklace. She was seen talking to

Elmar backstage. We searched the wagon, and found nothing."

Gray, seeing this was going to be a long conversation, decided to sit down in an unused, smelly chair.

"Gray and I will see what Elmar's show is all about. But first, I'd like to know how that couple with the pigeons made out. It's been a month or more since Edward Simpson came out to the ranch asking for my help. In that terrible storm, I put him on our mudwagon, found his mule, and brought them back to Bitter Wells. Is he okay?"

Tom raised his hand. "Yes, say no more. I know all about it. Your knowledge as to where to look for the people was correct. I led a posse right to the spot, and found two people huddled together in an old Conestoga wagon. The driver said his name was Abe Snowden, and his wife was Alma."

"The wheels of the wagon had broken through the ice into Red Cedar Creek. We tried to push the wagon out of the creek, but it wouldn't budge. It was too heavy. It took time to clear away all the snow, and unload the wagon. That's when I noticed an empty birdcage. When questioned, the man told me Edward Simpson, his son-in-law gave them a baby pigeon two years ago. He said he had put a message around the pigeon's foot, and released it, hoping it would find their home."

Tom took another long drag on the cigarette. "We tied all our ropes around the yoke of that wagon, and pulled it out with the help of all our horses. Then we reloaded their goods, and led them to town. Edward Simpson and his family were very happy to see his wife's parents. They said they were headed for Salt Lake City to deliver much needed medical supplies when the blizzard struck. Three days later the storm was gone, and the parents continued their journey. Right now, I'd bet the Simpsons are either at Elmar's stage or at the cookout we are having for Doc Markis."

"Yeah, Griff told me all about Doc Markis. It's a shame he is retiring, but Griff sent me into town for another reason. He wants me to find the thieves who slaughtered his ten cows."

"That was months ago, said a surprised Tom. "Their trail is cold. They're long gone."

"Yes, you could be right. I was busy with ranch repairs, and didn't have the time to look for them, but Griff still wants me to search for them. He believes I can still find them."

"That's a tall order. So what do you want me to do?"

"I understand you don't have the time to go after them so make me a deputy. I can go to the other counties with legal claim to what I am doing. I do not want to be thought of as a bounty hunter, or a gunfighter."

Joe took a step back from the desk as Sheriff Tom began to stand up. Both men were about the same height, but Gray could see Joe was the leaner and more agile of the two, even with a peg leg.

"Deputy, you say? That's how Griff is going to get even by using you? Are you ready for that, Joe? Peg leg and all?"

"Yes, I am, Sheriff Tom Howler. Put that damn badge on my chest, so I can be on my way."

Without any further hesitation, Tom reached into the desk drawer, and pulled out a badge. It was partly shiny with several scratch marks. He said a few words about the law, and then handed it to Joe. Joe hooked it to his shirt above his heart. Both shook hands.

"Now that you are my deputy for the short time you're in my town, you will do as I say. Understood?"

Joe nodded as he tipped his hat.

"You're a good man, Joe Lundy. Don't go beyond the law. I don't want to have to put you in jail."

Tom had an idea. He took a long puff on his cigarette, and sat down, grabbing a pile of posters. "Check out that snake oil guy, and make sure no drunks disturb the peace."

Joe turned, and started for the door. Gray rose out of his seat, and followed behind. He spoke not a word to the sheriff, but outside he did ask Joe if he could become a deputy someday.

Joe's reply was a sharp "No, you have to gain some experience first.

A tall man in a striped suit stood on the corner of the Snake Oil wagon. His fake, curly hair fluttered in the breeze as he held up a bottle that had a rose on its label. He, carefully, looked over the audience proclaiming. "Ladies and Gentlemen. My name is Elmar Root, and welcome to my show. For your pleasure, I have four young ladies that will sing and dance for you. Don't worry. It's free of charge, and they are not saloon girls, either. Also, I have the world's best fiddler, Jules Goldfine to entertain you. After the show, I want to tell you about a great new product I discovered, while we were in St. Louis, Missouri."

"So please enjoy our show, and later have a good dinner at Grannie's Store. I understand she's using this occasion to celebrate Doctor Markis' fiftieth birthday, so grab yourselves a good dinner after the show."

Elmar stepped onto the stage, and walked behind flap of the teepee. A moment of silence occurred, and then the audience could hear the strings of the violin playing Dixie. As the flap was pulled wide open, four lovely ladies dressed in white dresses, red roses in their hair, stepped forward, and began to swing their legs in time to the music. All of them had big smiles, and nodding to the audience.

A small, baldish man rapidly swinging the bow across his fiddle stepped out, and stood beside the ladies. He nodded to the audience too. For four minutes he played the tune encouraging the audience to sing along.

Jules pulled the bow across his fiddle one last time, and ended the song. People clapped as he stepped forward. He looked at the audience, bowed, and thanked everyone. He was the emcee, and opened with a bit of humor he said he picked up while visiting Mark Twain in California. The audience smiled. He continued his dialog for a few more minutes, and then he introduced one of the ladies. Her name was Blandina Downing. She stepped forward as Jules started playing a sweet love song. Her voice was soft but strong, and it created a mild echo off the side of Grannie's Store.

Joe and Gray moseyed around the back of Elmar's wagon. A woman with long brown hair, dressed in gray gingham was leaning against the driver's seat, watching the show.

Joe walked up to her. "Madam, are you looking for something?"

She turned and stared at both of them. She was upset. How could anybody disrupt her from watching the girl singing? Then she saw his badge. "What's wrong, deputy? I am just watching my daughter sing. Is there a problem with that?" She said curtly.

Joe thought she was acting a little too huffy, but he did not care. He was smitten. The woman now facing him was the loveliest female he had seen since his dear wife, Abbie. He had a hard time keeping his composure. He felt a sudden surge of pressure in his chest. He had to swallow hard to get the words out. "Sorry if we have bothered you. It is just we are new at this kind of work, and I am here to watch for any disturbances."

"Well, I am no disturbance, I hope."

Her daughter, Blandina, ended her song. "Can I ask what your name is?"

"My name is Sarah Downing." Being a little flippant, she asked what was his name.

"Joe Lundy."

Gray interjected. "Josiah Lundy, but everyone calls him just Joe." "Joe Lundy." I never forget a name. Excuse me."

Sarah climbed into the wagon, and greeted her daughter behind the stage. The teepee flap was closed, and both embraced. Joe stared at the flap, and then he and Gray walked toward Grannie's Store. Joe's heart kept thumping. He could barely hear Elmar's voice belting out his sales pitch about how good his snake oil product really was.

Inside the store, Joe could see Grannie had removed all her merchandise and had set up several tables. Each table was about ten feet long, and covered with a checkered cloth. Molly and her friends were serving the food. It was a raucous place with drinking and eating and loud chatter. One man was pulling his wife around while the children sat in wonder. The booze had got to him.

At first, Joe had to put his hands to his ears. He looked at Gray who stood motionless. "There's a table in the corner. Do you want something to eat?"

Gray gave a little nod. "Raw steak from a buffalo."

"Yes, but you're with me today. First, I have to do something."

Joe took his revolver out of his holster and fired two rounds into the rafters. Everyone stopped talking, and looked at Joe.

"I am your new deputy, and I am supposed to keep the peace. How come all of you scraggy men in work clothes eat like pigs, and beat your wives? Try to be kinder to your women who are so nicely dressed! You should show some respect for them as well as Doc Markis. So all of you hard working cowboys, take your beer or whiskey, and move to another table. Let the women sit together, and enjoy each other's company."

One big cowboy with a thick droopy mustache and unkempt beard stood up, and looked Joe square in the eyes. "Who are you to tell us where to sit? We have our women and kids. We do with them as we see fit. What do you have? A half breed?"

"I have a badge and a right to use it. I don't want any drunks disrupting today's celebrations. Understood?"

Joe put his arm around Gray's shoulder. "And that half breed as you call him is a full blooded Northern Ute who saved my life. Remember that!"

As Joe and Gray walked to the table in the corner, they could see all the men were carrying their plates and mugs of beer to a new location. By the time, Molly came and asked what they wanted to eat and drink, all the commotion had stopped temporarily, but then the noisy chatter started to pick up.

"What will you have?" a pert Molly asked.

"I will have a half done T-bone steak with all the fixins and a glass of beer," Joe replied.

He looked at his partner. "Gray what do you want to eat?"

"I want a buffalo steak, and a glass of sarsaparilla."

"How do you want your beef steak? They don't have buffalo here."

"Raw."

"Thank you." Molly winked at Joe, and strolled away. She liked helping out in Doc's celebration. Maybe, there was no money to be made, but she knew she would make up for it later in the night at Dave's Saloon.

Gray was impressed. "That was something how you settled everybody."

"It's all in your upbringing. My father controlled the family with a firm fist. You did something wrong, he used the belt on your butt as punishment. You did something right, he would say good boy, nothing more."

"And why did you ask for that awful stuff called sarsaparilla?"

"In Pennsylvania the people drink sarsaparilla and birch beer. They believe it's good for skin and blood problems. I smelled its odor once, and thought I would like to try it someday."

Molly returned. She placed the drinks on the table, and departed without saying a word.

Joe watched Gray as he took a sip of his drink. His face showed no emotion. Joe assumed he liked it. Joe raised his mug, nodded for Gray to do the same. The mugs touched. Joe said "Cheers," and took a long swig of beer.

Gray was mystified. "Why did you do that?" "You ask too many questions."

Gray noticed a man wearing a colorful bandana was coming their way. "Is that Rusty?"

Joe gave a slight nod as Rusty approached them. He was holding a plate with a huge sirloin steak on it in one hand, and a mug of beer in the other. "I saw you enter, and use your revolver.

The people were startled, that's for sure, but I was surprised how you handled that weapon of yours. There's a shooting match starting soon. Maybe you should enter. The prize is dinner for two at the Bitter Wells Café."

"Sit down and eat your steak, and stop giving me crap." Joe demanded. "I am getting better with my left hand, that's true, but there are people in this town who can shoot much better. I am sure of it."

Molly came to the table with two plates that were crammed with steaks and potatoes. "Here's your dinner, gentlemen."

Rusty stopped chewing on a piece of the steak, and looked up, straight into her eyes. She smiled, and gave him another seductive look.

"I will be over tonight around eight o'clock," he said.

"I'll be waiting," she said.

Someone at the next table yelled for more steak gravy. Molly turned away, and went to the kitchen area to get another bowlful.

After listening to the conversation between Rusty and Molly, Joe had to say something. "You know, Rusty, if you really like that woman, you should tell her before she gets tied up with somebody else. I bet if you got her away from her job of pleasing men at Dave's Saloon, you'd find she would make a wonderful wife. I have not known her very long, but I can see she is a good woman. Besides, you make enough money at the ranch; you could afford a spread of your own.

Don't be like Curley and Goldie who spend all their money on women, booze, and gambling."

Rusty finished eating. He stood up and grabbed his plate and mug. "You are right. I do like her a lot. I'm going into the kitchen, and tell her."

Rusty started to walk away, and then stopped. He looked back. "And don't you forget the shooting match."

A smiling, boastful Elmar jumped onto the stage, and announced, "Ladies and Gentlemen. I am sorry to tell you I have just sold the last bottle of my fabulous elixir, "Kentucky Dream. I know you will enjoy it. Now, I think it's time for our shooting match to begin. What do you say?"

Most of the audience smiled, some even clapped. All day long some of the men in the crowd had been placing bets with one of Elmar's workers. The stakes were high. Monte Dunham, son of the town's gunsmith, was the odds on favorite to win.

Elmar pointed to six men and two women standing next to his wagon. "Here are the best shooters your town has to offer. Which one will be the winner this year? Who will be given the honor of being named the champion of Bitter Wells? Let's give them a round of applause."

Elmar started to clap, and others joined in.

He pulled a coin out of his coat pocket, and held it high for everyone to see. "One last chance, my friends. Is there anyone else out there who would like to try his hand at winning this genuine gold piece? President Grant gave it to me years ago when I entertained him at the White House. It can be yours if you can score a complete bull's eye in any one of the three shooting stages. I remind you that nobody, in all the years I have been doing this show has been able to do it. No one!"

Elmar pointed to a wooden object next to the wagon wheel. "You, shooters don't have to worry. Whoever scores the highest number of hits after all three stages will take home that keg of my Kentucky Dream and the title of the Bitter Wells champion."

The audience clapped again.

Gray tapped Joe on the shoulder. "Why don't you enter?" He whispered.

"I told you my shooting is not as good as I'd like it to be." "What do you mean not as good?"

Joe pointed to the end of the crowd. "You see those two farm boys? They are from Santos' ranch, and I know they are very good shots. I've gone hunting with them. They don't miss. Their mother told me before their father died, he taught them much about guns. He was a crack shot in the Union Army. Once, while standing on a ridge in the Civil War, he killed a Confederate officer a mile away. I saw the medal to prove it."

Gray was insistent. "This is different. It is not a rifle match. It's a handgun match. I know you can do it. I have seen you shoot."

Someone standing behind them started talking. "Yes, why don't you try your luck? Let me see what you can do with that revolver of yours." Joe and Gray turned to see a smiling Sarah and her daughter, Blandina.

"Nice seeing you again." At first, they were all the words Joe could utter.

He studied the smiling faces of all three people, and knew he couldn't refuse. "Okay, I will do it, but Gray, you'll have to keep watch on the people in this town. I am still the deputy on duty."

"Blandina and I will be rooting for you. Good luck," said a friendly Sarah.

Joe walked over to Elmar. "I'd like to try my hand at this."

Elmar looked at the man facing him. He wondered how the hell this man with a hanging right hand and a peg leg could do anything.

"What does it cost?"

Elmar knew he did not want to take his man's money. "One silver dollar."

Joe's left hand produced a silver dollar, and tried to hand it to Elmar.

Elmar had to think fast. "Since you are a deputy in this town, I'll let you shoot free."

"Thanks," Joe said as he slipped the coin back into his hip pocket.

Elmar jumped off the stage, and led the people to an open space beside a large hay bale. One of the girl singers, carrying a ceramic bowl, was walking about twenty feet behind him. Gray surmised she must have been going to help Elmar. When Elmar stopped, she stopped too, and then took a medal disc, half the size of a silver dollar, out of the bowl, and held it up for all to see.

Elmar raised both arms. "Ladies and Gentlemen, please stand behind all the shooters. Thank you."

He pointed to his assistant. "You will see Lily is holding a metal item in her hand. It is called a slug. Gamblers use it in place of money in some remote mining camps. I say to you in our shooting match why ruin a good gold or silver coin? Not me, so I am going to use slugs for all three stages."

Elmar motioned to his assistant to flip the slug to him. He showed it to the shooters once again. "You'll see in the center is a small stamped red bull's eye. Lily, on my command, will throw this slug into the air. You must fire your gun and hit the slug before it touches the ground. In the first stage, if you hit any part of the slug, you will go on to the second event. If, by chance, you hit any part of the red bull's eye, you will skip the second stage, and go to the third and final one. Anyone who completely misses the slug is, of course, out of the competition. Lily will throw a new slug into the air for each shooter. Do all of you understand the rules?"

All the shooters agreed.

Elmar flipped the slug back to Lily.

"Good. Let's begin the first stage." "I'll let this young lady in a flowered dress go first."

She stepped forward; her hand was already on the holster. "What a pretty dress."

"Thank you."

"And what is your name?"

"My name is Emily." She seemed a little shy.

"Emily? That's a lovely name." I have a daughter in San Francisco I am hoping to see soon. She has the same name."

She smiled. "How old are you?" "I am fifteen today."

"Congratulations. I wish you the best." "Are you ready?"

"Yes."

Elmar pointed to his assistant. "I repeat once more. On my command, Lily will throw a slug into the air. You must draw and fire at the slug while it's in the air. You must hit the slug or you will be out of the match." He looked at Emily. "You do understand?"

Emily nodded. "I shoot rabbits and prairie dogs in our backyard all the time. I can do this."

Elmar stepped aside and yelled, "Throw the slug."

Emily's draw was fast. She had pulled the thirty-eight-caliber revolver out of its holster and fired three rounds. Lily found the slug and gave it to Elmar.

Elmar looked it over, and then showed it to Emily. There was no bullet marks anywhere on the slug. "Sorry, Emily, no hits, but you can keep the slug if you like."

She started to walk away saddened. Her mother embraced her, and then put her arm around her shoulders. They would not wait to see who would be the town's champion. They vanished into the crowd.

An older woman, Esther, dressed in buckskin, was next. She stated she had some shooting experience with a Texas road show. Lily threw the slug into the air, and Esther got off three shots. Elmar showed her the slug. She had hit a corner with one of her shots. She acknowledged it, and then she stepped back.

"Nice shooting, Esther. We'll see you in the second stage."

Out of six men entered, only two men, Monte Dunham and Dallas Grat were able to hit some part of the slug. No one, however, had hit any part of the bull's eye.

Joe stepped forward. Now it was his turn. Lily threw the slug high into the air, and Joe's left hand grabbed the revolver, pulled it out of the holster in lightning speed, and fired three times.

Lily picked up the slug, and handed it to Elmar. He held it up for everyone to see. "This man's bullet has gone through a part of the bull's eye, but I'm sorry to say, there are no other hits.

"Congratulations Joe. Good shooting. Because you did hit a part of the bull's eye, you will skip the second stage, and, later, go on to the third and final stage."

"And that's the end of the first event. Dallas and Esther have hit a slug, and Joe has hit a part of the bull's eye."

The bystanders applauded, and Joe, in his rather nonchalant way, stepped back. He just knew Gray and the two ladies must be pleased. He sure was.

Elmar was pleased too.

Now, Elmar turned to face the two remaining shooters. "Now, it's time for the second stage. All of you will be shooting at a much smaller slug this time. You must hit that slug to go on to the final stage. Are you ready?"

"Will Esther please step forward?" Ester nodded and said she was ready. Elmar yelled, "Throw the slug!"

Lily threw the slug high into the air, and Esther fired three rounds before it hit the ground. Lily found the slug and gave it to Elmar. He showed it to Ester. "Sorry, Esther."

She stepped back, but decided to stay to see who the winner would be.

"Monte Dunham. You're next."

A cocky, young man with long brown hair, stepped forward. "Save your breath. I understand the rules."

"Good." "Throw the slug." Yelled Elmar.

Lily threw the slug as high as she could, and Monte got off four shots before the slug hit the ground. Lily found the slug, and handed it to Elmar. He, in turn, showed it to Monte. There were no bullet marks in the slug.

"Sorry, kid. Better luck next time." "Don't call me kid!" He said, defiantly.

Monte stepped back, and threw his gun at the hay bale. He yelled a profanity, and marched off. Monte's girlfriend raced to the hay bale, and picked up the gun. She hurried to catch up to Monte who was heading straight for the saloon. She kept pleading with him not to go drinking again.

Dallas Grat stepped forward showing his calm demeanor. A highly polished Remington forty-five-caliber revolver was partly visible under the corner of his expensive dark blue blazer.

Joe noticed his revolver and had to make a comment. That's a good-looking piece of hardware you have."

Dallas pulled the Remington out of its snakeskin holster, and held up in plain view. "It has an eight inch barrel instead of the usual seven and a half inch one. Straighter fire power."

"Thanks for showing it to me," Joe said. "Now let's see what it can do."

Dallas replaced the revolver in its holster, and looked at Elmar. "I am ready. Throw that slug."

"Throw the slug!" yelled Elmar.

Lily threw the slug into the air, and it became caught in a sudden breeze, but that did not stop Dallas. He put his left hand on the firing arm, and fanned six rounds in rapid succession. The cool air caused some tiny puffs of smoke to rise from the barrel. Standing as proud as a peacock, he gently placed the Remington back in its holster.

Lily found the slug, and handed it to Elmar.

Elmar was quite impressed. One bullet had hit the corner of the slug, while another one had hit a part of the bull's eye. "Congratulations Dallas Grat. Good shooting."

"And that ends our second stage. Joe has one partial bull's eye, and Dallas has a partial bull's eye and two hits."

Elmar spoke loudly with high praise. "As everyone can see we have two very good shooters left, Joe Lundy, the town's deputy, and Dallas Grat, who told me earlier he is a gambler by trade."

As the audience applauded, a person came from Grannie's, and stood behind the crowd, watching the match.

"Now we will do the final stage." Elmar announced. "Lily, please set up a target in front of the hay bale."

She took one from behind the hay bale and placed it in front while Elmar explained the rules.

"Men." He pointed to the center of the target. "In front of that hay bale is a wooden target with two circles painted on it. The smallest circle is a half-inch in diameter and, of course, it is the bull's eye. The larger circle is two inches in diameter. When I yell shoot, you will draw your gun, and fire all six shots in rapid succession. You will be judged on how many hits you put completely inside the larger circle. No hits can touch the edge of the bull's eye. However, if you were to hit the bull's eye, dead center, you win that gold coin that I had mentioned earlier. When you are ready, nod, and I will yell "Shoot!." Do you understand?"

Both men nodded.

"Good. Let's begin with Joe this time."

Joe was becoming a little edgy. He was getting concerned about not performing his deputy duties. So before Elmar could yell "Shoot!" he quickly stepped forward and fanned his Smith and Westin revolver six times.

It took Elmar by surprise, but he said nothing. Lily brought the target to Elmar, and he carefully scrutinized the results. "Joe, you have five hits. All are in the two-inch circle, but no bull's eye. That gives you a total of five hits and a part of a bull's eye for a nice days work."

As Elmar faced the other man, Lily was already setting up a

new target.

"Dallas, will you now please step forward."

He stepped forward. He stood tall, his eyes concentrating on the target.

"You already have scored two hits and one partial bull's eye. You need three hits to tie, four hits to win." Elmar backed up a little scared. He imagined he could see the devil in Dallas's cold steel blue eyes.

Joe watched closely as Dallas drew his weapon and fanned it incredibly fast. The sound it made echoed off Elmar's wagon, and sounded like the army's Gatling gun.

Lily ran the target to Elmar. He scrutinized it carefully. He had a smile on his face as he looked up. "Dallas, you have two hits completely inside the larger circle, and, my, my, look at this, a perfect bull's eye."

Elmar stood up, pulled the gold coin out of his coat pocket, and presented it to Dallas. "You have won the gold coin fair and square. Great shooting." He gave Dallas the gold coin and shook his hand. A friendly crowd started forming around Dallas.

Joe tried to offer him a compliment. "Good shooting."

Dallas looked at Joe with a steady gaze. "This is not over. I have a gold coin, but I always want more. I know I'll be seeing you again."

Elmar spied Joe and Gray starting to walk away. "Joe, come back here. You won too."

Joe stopped as Elmar hurried toward him. "What do you mean I won? Won what?"

"You didn't get a bull's eye, but you had the most hits for the match. You have five hits to Dallas's four. Whoever had the most hits? That was the rules. You did it. You are the winner, and that keg of Kentucky Dream is yours," Elmar said as he tried to shake Joe's bad right hand.

Joe grabbed Elmar's arm with his left hand. "Thanks."

Gray, and the two women began congratulating Joe. He was taken back. "What am I going to do with a keg of Kentucky Dream?" he asked.

A face appeared from the back of the crowd. "Why not share it with your friends in this town. I am getting thirsty after watching you shoot." It was a smiling Sheriff Tom Howler.

"Hey, I'm sorry about not doing my duties as your deputy. Time got away from me."

"I know. I was here behind the crowd. My other deputy was keeping an eye on the town. Everything is fine. Enjoy yourself. Tomorrow is another day. Gotta go." Tom tipped his hat to the ladies, and headed back to the office.

"Gray, grab that keg and take it to Grannie's. We're going to have a party." He looked at Sarah and Blandina. "Would you like to come along?"

Laura said with a nice smile. "We'd love to."

Chapter

13

At the south end of Bitter Wells two people were strolling under a full moon. They came to a lonely tree. Both stopped. Sarah touched Joe's hand, and looked up into his eyes. Sarah was carrying a woolen blanket, while Joe had two. The summer's night was turning quite cool, but romance was in the air.

"Joe, let's you and me settle down under this tree. I brought some of your Kentucky Dream, some bread and cheese." She paused to look at the myriad of stars. "This night is ours to enjoy."

Joe spread one of his blankets out on a small plot of damp grass. Sarah sat down. She apologized for no picnic basket as she pulled a small flask, bread and cheese out of her two hip pockets, and laid them down. Joe unbuckled his holster, and laid it on the edge of the blanket as he sat down too. He was trying hard not to stare at the beautiful woman sitting next to him.

She broke the spell by picking up the flask, uncapping it, and handing it to Joe.

"I hope you do not mind drinking without glasses? I am usually more into proper etiquette, so please excuse me this time."

Joe took a swig. He knew he had to look into her eyes, the ones now glistening with a touch of moonlight. He couldn't help himself. He wanted to say something, but his words were a little hard to come by.

"Does the cat have your tongue?" Sarah smiled.

"No, madam." Joe swallowed. "It's been a long time since I had the honor of a female companion. A lovely one at that."

"Please call me by my name, Sarah. And I am honored to be with the champion shooter of Bitter Wells."

The silent spell on Joe was beginning to wane. He was beginning to feel a little more at ease. He wanted to sit closer to Sarah, but hesitated. He did not want to make her feel uncomfortable.

"I wonder what Blandina and Gray are doing? Do you think we should check on them?" a nervous Joe asked.

"Don't you worry about them! Blandina will keep Gray entertained. She knows I wanted to be with you alone."

"How did you come by naming your daughter, Blandina?" Joe blurted out.

"My husband named her after the Italian nun who opened schools and hospitals in the southwest. You know that woman once scolded Billy the Kid for his bad behavior."

It was Joe's turn to look up at the moon. "You are right. I didn't know this night was going to be so nice. What a party we had. That keg of Kentucky Dream lasted quite a while. Now, it's just you and me alone under the stars and moon."

"Yes, it has been a beautiful night."

"Joe, tell me something about yourself. How did you become such a good shooter?"

"As a young boy growing up on my mom's farm in Illinois, I had to supply the meat for our table. My father had a bad logging accident and died. I was thirteen years old, the oldest of three boys, and had to learn fast how to follow animal trails, and be a quick, accurate shooter. In time my mother met another farmer who was a widower, and she married again, so I joined the army. I scouted for them for years, and then tried to settle down until two men killed my wife and child."

"I am so sorry to hear that. You must have loved them very much." "Why do you have Gray as your sidekick?"

"Gray is about my age when I came west. I was alone and in need of a friend. During a blizzard that was coming in from the Rockies, I became snow blind. I was lost. An old mountain man found me, and took me to his cabin. I stayed with him for about two years before I went on my own. He taught me how to survive. I am Gray's mountain man for a while.

Sarah could sense Joe's sadness, so she changed topics. "Did you lose your leg when you were in the army?"

"No, I was driving cattle for the Delta D ranch when my horse and I fell down a steep arroyo. Griff and Amy Douglas, owners of the ranch, are good people. They gave me work and had their blacksmith make me a peg leg, which, I must say, works quite well. Enough about me, tell me about you and your cute daughter."

"Well, it's like this. We were living in Missouri. My husband worked on a paddle wheeler on the Mississippi River, and, one day, he passed out on the floor. The doctor told me he died from consumption. My Blandina was eight years old at the time. We sought comfort in our local church. Blandina would sing in the choir and the pastor was impressed. He told me Blandina's talent was too good to waste. Her voice was operatic. It was so strong. He said there was a good professional teacher in San Francisco, and I should take her there. He knew I had little money, so one Sunday he asked the church members if they would like to contribute money to help send Blandina and me to California."

"So why are you not on the train that runs through the next town, Miner's Creek?"

"The people in our church were poor too, and the money I received was only a small amount. I saw an ad in the St. Louis newspaper asking for singers. It read Elmar Root's Traveling Sideshow, heading west and in need of singers. I took Blandina to meet him at the dock. As he was about to board the ferry, I stopped him, and asked if my daughter could sing a few notes. At first, he refused but I kept pressuring him until he agreed to listen. Blandina sang just a few notes. He was so impressed, that he hired both of us. Blandina would sing, and I would help out with whatever was needed to be done."

"Didn't you have a home in Missouri?"

"No, we were renting. We were like sharecroppers, I suppose." Sarah broke the bread in half, and handed it to Joe. "Enough talk.

Let's eat a little."

Then she broke off a chunk of cheese, and handed it to Joe.

Joe could see a warmth and happiness in her manners and especially in those eyes. Together, they ate and drank in silence.

Then, Sarah decided to lie down on the blanket. She reached for Joe's arm. Joe took the hint, and lay down. He faced Sarah, his heart beating ever faster.

"Joe, when I saw you for the first time, I knew I wanted to be near you. I could see you are a strong but a gentle man who cares. That is what I like in a man."

Joe sighed a little. "Sarah, no woman has excited me more since my wife. I don't know if it is love at first sight, but I want to get to know you better."

Sarah gently caressed Joe's cheeks, and tickled his pencil moustache. Joe leaned closer. Their eyes met, and their sight faded away as they kissed passionately. A gentle breeze developed, and an owl hooted somewhere in the distance. Two people were becoming united as the hours drifted by.

Without warning, Joe heard footsteps coming their way. He reached for the other blanket, and in one full move had the blanket covering both of them.

"What's wrong?" A stunned Sarah whispered.

"Someone is coming." Joe reached for his revolver, and cocked the hammer. Sarah pushed the top of the blanket away as he sat up and pointed his gun.

Into the moonlight stood Gray and Blandina.

"You can put the gun away, Joe. We do you no harm," said Gray. Blandina spoke. "Mother, are you all right?" I was getting worried.

It's getting late, and Elmar wants everyone on board his wagon, and ready to leave early in the morning."

"Everything is just fine." She looked at Joe, and then at the two young ones. "Joe and I are going to sleep under the stars tonight. You go back to the wagon and tell Elmar I'll be there in the early morning. I'll be okay staying right here."

Joe spoke next. "Gray, you take our horses to the stable in town, and you tell the man I said to was okay for you to sleep in the loft. You might have to wake him up."

"But, Joe, I am supposed to be with you. That is my calling."

Joe was eager to end the conversation. "Sarah will stand in for you tonight. I'll see you tomorrow at Elmar's wagon. Everything is good."

"Yes, I understand." Both Gray and Blandina looked at each other and smiled. Gray thought white man very strange sometimes. A man in this tribe takes a woman to be his bride, and sleeps inside teepees, not outside.

Chapter

14

Blandina jumped off the wagon, and rushed toward Sarah and Joe. "Mother, Elmar is very anxious to leave. Everyone is aboard. We must hurry."

She took the three wool blankets out of her mother's hands, and gave her a knitted shawl. "It's a little chilly right now. Please wear this for a while until the sun warms the air."

Sarah smiled as she draped the shawl around her shoulders." I will be with all of you soon, I promise, but first, I have to say my goodbyes to Joe."

"Okay, but hurry." Blandina turned, and hurried back. A young man standing in the wagon reached for her hand, and lifted her aboard.

Sarah turned to face Joe for the last time. "I had a wonderful time; watching you win the shooting match, the wonderful party we had with your friends, and especially our time alone. I will always remember, and cherish it."

"I know Blandina had a good time too. She'll tell me all about it once the wagon gets rolling. I know she liked Gray. I could see it in her eyes. It's so sad to leave this town and especially you."

She reached for Joe's hands. She squeezed them tightly. She stood on her toes and looked into his eyes. Joe, I have known you just one day, a wonderful day it was, and now my heart aches because I have to say goodbye. You are my kind of man. Don't you ever forget it. Okay?"

Joe felt a sadness growing deep inside.

Oh, hogwash, he thought. He could not help himself. A tear formed, and trickled down his cheek. "Sarah, I will miss you also" He wiped the tear away, and planted a deep kiss on Sarah's lips. "I wish you would reconsider staying around here. I could get you a job. There's a lady in the boarding house in our town who plays the piano. She could teach Blandina."

Sarah, with tears flowing from both eyes, leaned against Joe's chest, and whispered, "I promised Blandina I would get her a professional teacher. One who could train her voice, and help her to be a success in a famous opera house. That is what I am going to do. I am sorry, Joe, I love you. I know it, but my word comes first."

Joe truly understood. He reached down, picked up Sarah, cradled her in his arms, and then started walking toward the wagon. By the wagon's side, he stopped, gave her a farewell kiss, and lifted her onto the wagon bed. He tipped his Stetson, said a soft goodbye, stepping back, as the wagon began pulling away.

Sarah leaned over the side, and yelled. "If you ever get to San Francisco please look for me. I will be waiting, my love."

Joe waved a little. He stood there, and he felt alone. He knew the feeling all too well.

"Did my friend have a good night's sleep?"

A startled Joe turned. Gray had quietly appeared out of nowhere. "Are you ready to hit the trail?" He said. His face displayed no emotions, but Joe could see his wry humor. Joe knew all along Gray must have had some feelings hidden behind those dark eyes.

Joe reacted. "Don't call me your friend! Can't you see I'm upset? I just lost the love of my life."

He noticed a paisley printed bandana draped around Gray's neck. "Where did you get that damn thing that's around your neck?"

"Do you like it? Blandina gave it to me. I love it. She is a fine person."

"It's ugly. I'll buy you a better one."

"No, you will not. Blandina is the first woman to give me such a nice gift. I will keep it forever, as you white people might say."

"Okay. You keep it, but don't come crying to me when some drunk calls you a girl and tries to knock your head off."

"I will not let that drunk touch my bandana. I will show him the point of my knife."

"You do that, and you'll sit your ass in jail until the sheriff gets the noose ready. I thought I have taught you better than that. Use the whip I gave you. I know you have been practicing with it for months."

"I might just do that."

Both sensed movement. They looked back to see someone was heading their way, and in a big hurry.

It was Jessip. He stopped in front of Joe, trying to catch his breath. "Deputy Joe, there is an angry man trying to rob the saloon. I think he stabbed the bartender, and he won't leave."

"Where is the sheriff or his deputy?"

"Sheriff Tom and Ray are out of the office. The incoming stagecoach was about two miles out when it lost a wheel. Tom is bringing a new wheel to the driver. He wants to make sure the passengers are safe, and not hurt.

"Why is Ray with him?"

"There a strongbox of gold aboard that is for our bank. Tom wanted extra protection, just in case."

"Thanks Jessip. I'll get right on it. Gray, get my whip off the saddle, and meet me at Dave's Saloon."

Gray was fleet of foot. He went to the stable, grabbed both Joe's whip and his, and made it to the saloon door before Joe.

Joe yanked his whip out of Gray's hands. "You stay here, and watch how I handle a drunken robber. You are not allowed in this place. Stay here, and have your whip ready in case he has a partner. I don't need any more trouble than one hombre at a time."

Gray nodded as Joe pushed the saloon doors wide open with his right forearm, and held his whip ready for action in his left hand.

He placed his peg leg inside the saloon first, and then the left leg. He surveyed the entire room. Most of the early drinkers had disappeared. Several card tables were upside down or broken into halves. Playing cards and coins were strewn about. The floor was wet in places, and it reeked of the smell of beer. At the bar a huge fellow dressed in only a dirty, tattered shirt who was threatening the bartender. He was barefooted, and as big as an ox.

As Joe walked closer, the man made no attempt to see who was behind him. In a loud outburst of anger, he grabbed the neck of an empty whiskey bottle lying on the bar, and broke it in two. He raised it high and was about to hit the bartender on the head. He kept yelling profanities, and demanding all the money that was in the safe.

Joe, acting as calm as can be, stepped forward, raised his whip, and cracked it across the man's hand. The bottle flew over the bar. The man started screaming in pain as he turned to face his new enemy.

"What the hell are you doing? You could have broken my right hand." He snarled. "You think you're some big jackass, don't you? Hidin' behind that tin badge? I'll pick you up with my other hand, and squeeze the crap out of that pretty neck of yours."

"I wouldn't try that if I were you. My whip has more power in it than that giant paw of yours or that old side arm you are carrying."

"You are standing in my way. I want all the money that's in the safe. The bartender says he doesn't know the combination. That's bullshit. I saw him earlier open it."

"What do you need the money for? There is a bank down the street. Try robbing that one."

"Oh, now you're a wise jackass. Now you are really asking for it." "Stay where you are!" Joe demanded.

"Bullshit."

It was no use. The giant, bearded, half-naked man lunged at Joe much like a vicious bull in a Mexican arena. His two outstretched hands looked like the horns of El Toro.

Joe flicked his wrist again. This time the whip broke the wrist bones in his other hand. Joe stepped aside as the man issuing terrible screams rushed out of the saloon. Gray used his whip to lasso the man's legs, and watched as he tumbled off the wooden sidewalk. He landed facedown in the street. He did not move.

Joe looked at the bartender. "Are you going to be okay?"

"Yeah, I guess so. I'll get the doctor to care for the wounds on my head and arms. I want to thank you, Joe. Everyone in this saloon was afraid of that guy. He acts like a big old Grizzly bear."

"What does he do for work?"

"He sells salt to the Mexicans down south, and comes into our town once in a while. He drinks like a fool, and looks for a fight. I've decided I am going to stop handling people's money accounts, and let the bank do it. It will be cheaper for me."

"Good idea. You won't need me quite as often."

Joe started to exit the saloon. He stopped, pulled out of his pocket a silver coin, and flipped it to the bartender. "Maybe this will help pay for some of the damage."

As he pushed open the swinging doors, he saw Gray tying a rope around the unconscious man's hands. "Where did you get the rope?"

Gray looked up. "Off that horse over there. You really messed up this man's hands."

"No need to worry. He'll sit his ass in a jail cell, and the doctor will look at them. By the time he is released, his hands will be mended. Maybe, not as well as before, but they will be workable."

Joe signaled to two bystanders who were watching from the other side of the street to come over. "Help us get this galoot to the jail, so you can go back to your card games."

With one person at each arm and leg, they dragged the man

two blocks to the jail in the sheriff's office.

Tom came riding into town and looped the reins of his horse around the hitching post. He noticed some drag marks and a trail of blood in the street. When he opened the office door, he saw Gray sitting on the floor, and Joe was interrogating a prisoner. Jessip was nearby jotting down notes. He couldn't help to notice the stench coming from the drunken prisoner.

"I see you got yourself a prisoner. What is he in for?" Joe turned and said, "Oh, about five years, I'd say."

"Five years screamed the prisoner. He went into a rage. Holding his hands by his side, he rammed his body into the bars. "You can't hold me for that long!" The man rammed the bars again, and spit at Joe. He remembered how much pain he felt in his hands. "I'll get you! You slick, smooth talking son-of-a bitch!"

"That will be enough. I don't want to hear any cussin' in my office. Understand?" Tom meant every word he said, and the man seemed to know it.

Joe asked, "Where is Ray?

"He is riding shotgun to make sure the stage gets here."

The man sat down on the cot, and relented some. "Okay. Let's talk. This place gives me the willies. I'm used to being alone in the desert, not in here, caged up like an animal."

"You better get used to it." Tom warned.

"Tom, what's the penalty for trying to steal the saloon's money, breaking the furniture and cutting the bartender?"

Tom touched his chin and thought. "I'd say he should get ten years for trying to rob a bank, and pay all other expenses. You agree?"

Joe nodded as the man shouted again. "I didn't rob a bank! You can't get me for that! It was a saloon that owned me a lot of money!"

Tom replied, "What's your name?" The man slumped back

unto the cot.

Tom raised his voice. "Well, whatever your name is, I am telling you several of the townspeople still keep their savings in the saloon for safekeeping. They don't trust the new bank we have now. That will change in the future, but for right now you are facing bank robbery charges."

"What's wrong with you?" Joe asked. "What's bothering you or are you just plain nuts? You sit there naked as a jaybird except for that dirty shirt. Did you smoke some Indian peyote?"

The man tore off the ragged deer hide shirt. He turned his back to Joe and Tom. "You see those deep cuts? You see all of them? Fifteen desperados took turns doing it. They spoke mostly Spanish, and smelled to high heaven like me. I was crossing the basin with a load of salt, and they said I got in their way."

Joe questioned. "So what does that have to do with robbing our saloon?"

The man was frustrated. He put his head between his hands, and sobbed. "One hombre spoke a little English. He pointed to a brown packhorse. He said they were going to open the strongbox that is on its back, and fill their saddlebags with all the gold. Then we would put it in the saloon in Bitter Wells for safekeeping. No one would be the wiser. Later, they will back for it when things quieted down."

"I asked where did they get the strongbox! The hombre smiled and showed me his rotten teeth. He said they robbed a stagecoach heading to Mexico. They killed the driver and all the passengers. He laughed, and then he said I must die too."

"That's a good story," Tom said. He looked at Joe. "Yesterday, I got a message from the telegraph office saying a stage was going to Mexico City, but it never made it."

Joe looked at the man. "So why rob the saloon?"

"I lost everything. I had one hundred pounds of salt on my burro and twenty silver coins in my pocket." He showed them his feet. They were scarred and blistered. "They took my boots, my knife and revolver, even my shirt and pants. They thought I would die from the sun," He pointed his forefinger at Joe. "But I fooled them. By good fortune, I came upon an abandoned shack, and that's where I got this shirt and that old revolver. I didn't have any bullets for it. I walked for days till I came to this town this morning."

Joe was getting impatient. "Why the saloon?"

"I wanted to get all that gold they gave to the saloon. I felt I was entitled to it."

Tom said, "Well, you're not entitled to it, even if we did have it. Besides, the bartender would have told me if anyone gave him any large amounts of gold. He would have reported it to me right away." He yelled at the man. "No gold, you fool!"

Joe tried to offer solace. "If you tell us your name, and work to pay for all the damage you have done, the judge might go easy on you. Think it over."

As Joe and Tom started to walk into the office, the man stated. "My name is "You boy."

"You boy? What kind of name is that?" Joe wondered.

"I was an orphan living in Abilene, Kansas. I never knew my parents. I roamed the streets searching for food. I didn't even know my real name. People would say you boy, get me this or get me that. I would do it and they would give me some food or money, so I called myself, "You boy." I can't read or write. My signature is a X."

"Okay, You boy. Settle down. Get some rest." A softer Joe offered. "And take the blanket off the bed and cover yourself. We have respectable people come by once in a while. Who wants to see that big totem pole of yours?"

Jessip blushed as he closed his note pad, rushed straight outside, and across the street. He knew he had a good story worth a few extra coins.

Inside the office, Joe could see Gray sitting on the floor playing with his little bag of stones. Gray looked up. He had a worried look on his face.

Joe was annoyed. "Forget those stupid stones. We have work to do."

Gray felt he had reasons to be concerned. The stones told him a deadly thing was soon to happen, maybe in three moons or so. He put the stones back in the bag, stood up, and started to follow Joe.

Somebody from the outside pushed the office door open, and started forcing his way in. It was the Edward, the telegraph operator. Joe could see he was in a rush, so he and Gray stepped aside to let him pass.

Tom looked up as he started to light his cigarette. "What's up, Edward?"

"Tom, you asked me to tell you if someone knew where those two men, Jonas and Zach, were."

"Yes, where are they?"

"I just received a message from the sheriff in Stampede. He says those men were drunk last night, and are locked up in his jail for disturbing the peace. He said he couldn't hold them too long, maybe a day or two at the most. You must hurry."

"Thanks, Edward."

Edward backed up, and turned toward the door.

"It's good to see you again. How are you?" Joe smiled a little as he reached in his shirt pocket for a cigarette.

"Just fine," Edward said as he passed by and went out the door. "Edward seems as nervous as Jessip," Joe remarked to Tom.

"He gets that way sometimes, but not as bad as Jessip. I had told him we needed to know the whereabouts of those two men, Zach and Jonas, as soon as possible. You see the results. He's a good man."

Joe looked at Gray as he took a drag on the cigarette. "I think you know where we are headed next. Did your stones tell you that?"

Gray said nothing.

"Get your gear and saddle up the horses. It's quite a ways to Stampede."

Joe turned to Tom. "We should be back in three days with our prisoners."

"Watch out. Those men have left a bad trail of greed and killing."

Tom warned. "The sheriff in that town is young, but a good, honest man. He should be able to help you."

Joe nodded a little with a small smirk on his face. "Adios."

Chapter

15

Stampede was partly a ghost town since the silver mines petered out. One half of it looked like a series of large children's blocks strung together with chains. Their construction consisted of rotting wood and dried mud; the chains had been installed to keep the square shaped buildings from flying apart in a sudden twister. The other end of town consisted of charred remains of fancy homes and empty corrals. In the distance, one could see the silhouettes of rusted machinery, and a couple of dilapidated buildings used for smelting. Mining holes dotted the surrounding hills.

As Joe and Gray slowly rode their horses into the town, they noticed a sheriff's sign firmly attached to the front of the second square building. There was no porch or curtains to keep the sun from pouring in through a small, busted front window. There were only a few boards lying on the ground in front of the door, no sidewalks anywhere.

Gray looked at Joe. "Leader, this place looks awful. Who would want to live here? My tribe calls this place the belly of the coyote, not a good place for people."

"Gray, don't call me Leader again. You know my name." "I forgot. I was thinking about my vision."

"Okay, but keep an eye out for those two men that we are after. They could have broken out of jail, hiding behind one of these buildings, waiting to ambush us."

They saw a pole protruding from the front wall, so they dismounted, and tied their reins to it. Joe, with his left hand on his holster, could see the door was ajar. He pushed it completely open, and peered inside. Except for a single beam of sunlight, the inside looked dark and dusty like no one had lived there for years.

As Joe started to enter, he felt the barrel of a gun pressing against his back.

"Drop your gun, and turn around slowly. And I do mean slowly."

Joe dropped his gun. He and Gray turned around to face their adversary. He was a lanky, six foot two inch young man with a blond mop of hair, holding a loaded Winchester '73.

First, Joe looked down at Gray with displeasure. How could you not have warned me?" he said to himself.

Joe spoke to the man with firmness in his voice. "I am Joe Lundy, the deputy from Bitter Wells. My partner is Gray, a Ute. We are here to get the two men you have in your jail."

The man was not convinced. He had seen too many holdups recently. People were robbing each other to stay alive. "Where's your badge?"

"It's in my shirt pocket."

"Show me, but take it out, nice and easy." Joe presented the badge.

The man relaxed his grip on the rifle. "I'm Wil Abrams, the sheriff in this town, if you can call it that."

He reached out to shake their hands. "Sorry, but I can't be too careful. I overheard the men in my jail talking about their friends who were coming to get them out. If their friends are as bad as what I hear about Zach and Jonas, I would be unable to handle it. Thank God you will be taking them with you."

Wil looked down at Gray. "Do the two of you think you can handle them? It's a long trip back to Bitter Wells."

Joe looked Wil square in the eye. "Don't worry. You give us these so called bad guys, and we'll be on our way."

Wil pointed to another building. "Over there is my office and sometimes my home when the wife gets mad at me. I had to move out of this one because the scorpions were taking it over. The ones around here are big and mean bastards too. Tried eating them once, but they don't taste too good."

"Follow me."

As they walked, Gray was curious and wanted to know what

happened to this weird town and who lives here now.

Wil was only too happy to comply. "I'll tell you. I grew up here. Many years ago a mysterious mountain man came this way. He never gave his name and was almost killed by a herd of stampeding buffalo. He said a violent wind must have spooked the animals, and that's how this town got its name. That man found little cover and was trampled upon. He managed to live, and stayed here to recover. In one of the ruts the buffaloes had made, he found a rock containing silver." Wil pointed down the street. "You see that pile of rocks down there next to our well? He did that to mark the location, so he could find this place when he returned. Sad to say, he never returned. A roving band of Mexican banditos killed him. But he was able to tell a friend what he had found. That friend brought many miners with him, and they dug lots of silver out of the hills around here. When the silver petered out, most of the miners moved on, but a few decided to stay, and started raising sheep and goats."

Wil stopped at the office door, and pointed to the rest of the town. The people, who owned the mines lived in fancy homes. The poor people couldn't stand their high-fallutin' ways, and chased them out. Then, they burned their homes down for good measure. It's sad to say that because we could have used the lumber."

He opened the door. "C'mon in."

Joe and Gray stepped inside. They could see the office was smaller than Tom's, in Bitter Wells, but a lot cleaner. A potbelly stove sat directly in the middle of the room. Joe noticed a telegraph key on his desk, and a spittoon next to a leg of the desk.

"Take a seat. We'll get down to business a little later. Zach and Jonas are going nowhere. There are locked up in the next building that's tighter than a sardine can."

"I see you must work the telegraph?" Joe asked.

"Yeah, my wife helps out sometimes. We get very few visitors around here, so the telegraph is our only way to get the latest news."

Wil pulled a cigar out of his top desk drawer and lit it. "I do believe in hospitality. I'll have my woman bring us a pot of tumbleweed soup and a pitcher of goat's milk.

Joe was a little edgy. He wanted to get under way as soon as possible, but he didn't want to annoy the sheriff. I instead, he asked, "What do you smoke?"

Wil replied, "I like those big Cuban cigars. It's my one treat twice a year when our neighbors go into your town for food and Christmas supplies."

Joe reached his shirt pocket, and pulled out the fixings to make his own cigarette. "We can't stay too long. I want to get back to Bitter Wells before dark."

"I understand."

Wil stood, grabbing his rifle. He walked outside, and fired a shot in the air. Then he came back inside, and settled back in his chair, a trail of cigar smoke followed him in.

He looked at his two surprised guests. "Oh, that's my signal to bring over the food."

A short, stocky woman in a plain gingham dress came inside the office, and placed a pot of soup and a gallon jug of goat's milk on the sheriff's desk. She pulled out of her hip pocket a small loaf of dark bread. Behind her was a small child also wearing a plain gingham dress. The youngster was carrying cups and bowls and spoons, and placed them on the desk.

"This is my wife of six years, and my daughter of seven years. Marie and I had to wait until our daughter, Lily, was born before we got married. Although not accepted by the Mormons it's the custom of the Abrams clan."

Marie was silent but nodded her greeting. Lily did likewise, and both hurried out the door.

"You have a nice family," Gray said.

"Well, thank you, you little vermin," Wil replied. "His name is Gray," Joe firmly answered back.

"Oh, I meant him no harm. I call my favorite nephew a little vermin, and he is eighteen years old."

Wil spooned out the soup, and poured the goat's milk into the cups. Joe and Gray watched as Wil said a quick prayer. Then, all began to eat.

"This soup is quite good," remarked Joe. "How does your wife make it?"

"She gets the green stems from the tumbleweed before it gets too old. She cuts it up in pieces, pounds it with a hammer. She adds it to a pot of wild fowl broth, and a few secret spices. She won't tell anybody what those spices are."

"The goat's milk is cold," Gray said. "How do you do that?"

"Marie will collect the milk into an eared jug, and plug it with a tapered pin I made her. Then, she will tie a rope to the ears of the jug, and lower it into the well. The well water is ten feet down, and it is always running. To where I don't know, but it keeps the milk good and cold. Sometimes, Marie will bring me a couple of bottles of beer from your town, and I lower them in the well too."

"Do you plan to move away sometime?" asked Joe. "There's some good grazing over the mountains. Some of our townsfolk have already moved there."

"No, I doubt it. Our families have worked hard to build this place. Maybe to some people it doesn't look like much but to us it's our home."

When the meal was over, Joe looked at Gray, then at Wil. "I want to thank you for your hospitality as you call it. It was good. Now, I need to get the prisoners."

Wil acknowledged Joe's need, and all three stood up. Wil led them outside and to the next building. "I put a lot of barbed wire around the outside of this building. It keeps the foxes out and the drunkards in."

He unlocked the door, and all three went inside.

It stank to high heaven. Joe winced and Gray covered his nose with the bandana Blandina had given him. It did no good.

Wil saw Gray's reaction. "I know it smells like shit in here. It's because these two so-called men have no other place to do their crap. After they leave, Marie and Lily will clean the place out, and to ready for the next rowdy bunch that comes through here."

Wil led them to the iron bars that divided the room. Two scurvy looking' messed up bums all covered in feces were laying on the floor, half asleep.

Wil pointed. "Here are the men you are looking for."

Joe rubbed the ends of his mustache, walked up to the bars, and then he shouted. "Get your damn asses up off the floor now, or I will blow a hole through both of you right here and now.

Both men quickly arose, and stared at Joe. The one with wild red hair and a long beard that went down to his belly button looked at Gray. "What's that fuckin Indian doing here? Give me a gun and I'll shoot the bastard."

"You'll shoot nobody. When you outside, I'll make you regret those words." Joe declared.

The man knew better. He fell silent.

Joe signaled to Gray to go outside. Wil and Joe followed. Outside, all breathed a sigh of relief'

Joe looked at Wil. "They are not Zach and Jonas. I worked with them for a few years punching cows."

"They said they were Zach Reis and Jonas Diver."

"Well, they are not. You have the wrong men. And boy, do they stink! Didn't you look at the wanted poster?"

"I didn't have a poster, only the telegraph message from Bitter Wells. I took these guys at their word."

Wil was dismayed. "Wait here."

He went back inside. Gray and Joe could hear some shouting and roughhousing, then silence.

Wil came out, and presented a folded note to Joe.

As he opened the note, he could smell the stench. It was almost too overpowering, but Joe persisted to read what it had to say. When he was finished, he held the note in his outstretched hand away from his body, and spoke directly to Wil. "This note is written by someone who has some education. Zach and Jonas could barely write their own name. If the two men you have in jails are not smart enough to write it, then who?"

"First, what did the note say?" Wil asked. "I can read only a little."

"It said Zach and Jonas knew we would be coming, and decided to stay one step ahead of us. They paid those drunken men to pretend to take their name. Then, they hightailed out of here with your niece. I can see this is becoming a game with them."

"So those two bastards I have locked up ate my food, and slept in my jail for free. Son-of-bitches." Wil was getting madder. It appeared he was showing more interest in his jail than his niece.

"Calm down, friend. Nobody was harmed, were they?" "Yeah, but someone might have been." Wil looked lost.

"Who is that?"

"It's my niece, Alice."

"There were two men who came by here, looking for a drink of water."

"Was one of them a short person who liked flashing a shiny butcher's knife?" asked Joe.

"Yes, I remember. He said he liked to pick his teeth with it." "That was Zach, and the other guy was Jonas, I bet." Joe added.

"Well, isn't it odd to allow a strangers to take your niece away?" Joe wondered.

"Alice said she wanted to go with them. Since there are so few eligible men around here we allowed her to go. Besides, she had no father or mother. Both died of consumption."

"Well, tell me. What town did they go to?"

"They told me they were going to Miner's Creek. He even threw a few gold coins my way. Said it was partial payment for my niece's hand."

Joe thought hard. "There is no place in Miner's Creek where you could buy a wedding dress. It has cheap bars and nothing more. The closest place I know is Soledad City, and that's eighty miles north from here."

Gray spoke to Joe. Are you saying we are going to Soledad City, not Miner's Creek? We can't make it before night."

"You can bed down in my office tonight." Wil offered.

Joe started walking to his horse. "No thanks, we need to get started now, so we can catch up to them."

Joe looked back at Gray. "I'm afraid we will be sleeping under the stars tonight."

Joe musingly added. "Or you could stay here in the jail until I return."

A stoic Gray said, "No, I must go where you go until my vision is complete."

Wil was lost. "What vision? What are you talking about? And what am I going to do with those men locked in my jail?"

Joe smiled as he mounted his horse, and steered away." Make them clean the jail, then kick their asses out of your town. I'll be back with your niece soon."

Gray climbed into his saddle. Together, they galloped out of town.

Chapter

16

The darkness was falling fast. Gray spied a group of trees next to a small stream just off the trail.

"Joe, can we stop under one of those trees just ahead? My horse is getting tired, and thirsty."

Joe smiled to himself. He knew Gray was not used to sitting in the saddle on long trips, and that it was the rider who was getting tired and thirsty.

"Okay, partner, I can see your horse needs to rest," Joe said jokingly. "How ''bout we get a few hours of shut eye, then get an early start in the morning?"

"Okay, Joe."

When they did stop next to the Big tooth maple, Gray was the first to dismount. He landed on his feet, trying to get the kinks out of both his back and legs. He wobbled a little, while he rubbed his buttocks.

Joe watched, but said nothing. He dismounted, and tied the reins of his horse to a branch. He headed to the stream where he knelt down, laying his hat on the ground. Then, he cupped his left hand, and scooped up some water. He could feel its coolness, its taste. He repeated this until his thirst was satisfied, and then dunked his head deep into the babbling water. Feeling refreshed, he grabbed his hat, stood up, and started back to the tree.

Gray was just standing, rubbing his horse's neck.

"What in tarnation are you waiting for? I thought your horse was thirsty! Go! Get the water from the stream. And when you're finished find some wood, so I can start a fire."

Gray said nothing. He walked his horse to the stream. Both the horse, and he lapped up some water. To Gray, it felt good. It was so cool and comforting going down his parched throat. He took off the paisley bandana, wetted it, and rubbed his face and head.

It felt cool and comforting as well. Then, he wrapped and tied the wet bandana around his neck.

Gray grabbed the horse's reins as he looked up at the myriad of stars. They were starting to twinkle, and seemed to greet him. The shimmering light from the half moon seemed to say hi. Gray felt awed, and inspired. He just could feel the time was fast approaching when he would get that gray owl feather he so desperately wanted, and then, he could be headed back to his tribe, and to his future wife. Gray touched the little bag of stones that now he kept under his armpit, just like his hero, Crazy Horse would have done. The stones never lied, he strongly believed.

Gray turned, and started picking up twigs as he led his horse back to the tree. Joe was getting something out of his saddlebag.

"Are you not going to take Rain to the stream?" he questioned.

"No, Rain already had his drink." Gray was confused. "How did you do that? You were not beside me?"

"Rain likes me to pour the water from my canteen into its mouth. He thinks he deserves it, I guess. If he wants more he will let me know. In the morning, I will refill my canteen."

Gray did not answer, but thought once again these white people have strange ways of doing things. He unhitched the saddle, placed it on the ground, and laid out his bedroll. He thought he was set for the night.

Joe held up two strips of food. "See this? He pointed to the first one. "This is beef jerky, all two pounds of it. Then, he held up the second one. "See this? This is two pounds of pemmican. I am going to cut both of them in half, and save some for our trip back to Stampede."

Next, Joe reached into his shirt pocket, and pulled out a small cloth bag. "I have some herbs Amy gave me, and I am going to rub them all over the beef jerky. I want a big fire to cook them on. These little twigs you brought won't last. I need bigger ones now."

Gray understood the word "Now." He arose, and quickly found several larger pieces of wood nearby. Joe, using his skills as a frontiersman, had a good blaze going in no time.

The darkness of the night was complete except for the glow of the fire.

Both ate their fill, and reclined against their saddles.

Gray said, "The meat was real good. I like the taste of the herbs." "Amy wouldn't tell me what they were. All she said was she grew

them in Kentucky years ago, and dried them out. She stored them in a jar, and brought them out west. You can't find them in Bitter Wells. I know that for sure. Grannie claimed she never in her born days had she seen anything like it."

The flames of the fire dwindled, and a chill could be felt. Gray covered himself with a blanket. "I'll see you in the morning."

It was time for Joe to light up his evening smoke. He pulled a cigarette out of his other shirt pocket. He lit it up, leaned back, and gazed at the stars. "Okay, Gray. See you early tomorrow," he said softly.

Minutes passed. All was quiet except the screech of an owl in one of the trees on the other side of the stream. Life seemed idyllic.

Then as Joe finished taking the last puff on his cigarette, he thought he heard a noise coming from across the stream. He listened for a few seconds. He focused his mind, and listened intently. Yes, it was a noise, he determined, a noise he didn't like, and it was getting louder and louder. Joe knew it was coming his way.

Joe pulled his revolver out of his holster. He reached over, tapped Gray on the shoulder with his bad hand. "There's something coming in our direction. I can't be sure what it is, so just sit still. The fire is almost out, but we might see what it is in the moonlight."

Gray sat motionless as the seconds passed by. Joe had the barrel of his revolver pointed straight ahead.

The noise became a rambling sound that turned into a splash, followed by a series of grunts. Joe knew whatever it was had just crossed over the stream and was headed their way, for sure. He cocked the hammer, and studied his aim.

He saw nothing, but a mass of hair swaying in the moonlight.

Whatever it was, Joe knew it had to be big, very big, and hungry.

Suddenly, the beast loomed in front of the dying fire, but it stopped, and started sniffing the hot embers. It was the biggest grizzly bear Joe had ever seen. Its eyes picked up the glow of the embers. They were piercing dark brown. It looked real mean, real mean. Then, it bared its two massive front teeth. Joe knew his gun would be of little use. He waited. Gray froze.

Soon, Joe began to realize there was something different about this bear. It just stood there, continually sniffing all the hot embers. Joe began to see what was going on. This bear didn't want to attack them. It wanted their food. He knew bears have a great sense of smell, and this one must have picked up the aroma of the meat Joe had roasted.

Joe wasted no time. He slowly pulled out of his saddlebag the remaining piece of pemmican, and threw it at the Grizzly's feet.

The grizzly sniffed it, let out a roar as only a grizzly can, picked up the pemmican, and scampered back across the stream. It disappeared into the trees.

A scared but elated Gray said, "Joe, you sure knew what to do with that bear. I thought we were going to be attacked." Gray touched the stones in his bag once again.

"I could see that bear was not a killer. It smelled our food, and wanted some. Somebody must have trained it. It was used to being around people. Let's get some shut eye."

"I hope you are right. I don't want to be its next meal," Gray said.

Joe grabbed his blanket, and covered himself. As he drifted off to sleep, Gray stayed awake, still a little scared.

Gray watched some clouds come out of nowhere, and drift passed the moon. He did not know how long he was awake, but there it was again. Not the sounds of the bear this time, but the occasional ringing of a bell. It was just like the sound of the bell on the prospector's donkey. Could it be the same one? He asked himself. He did not want to wake up Joe, but he felt he had no choice.

He tapped Joe on the shoulder. "Joe, I hear a new sound. It sounds like the bell that the prospector had on his donkey. I think it's coming our way."

Joe pushed the blanket aside. "You weren't dreaming were you? I don't hear . . ."

The sound was real. Joe reached once again for his gun, and cocked the hammer. "Looks like we are not getting any sleep tonight. This tree we are under must be a meeting place of some kind."

The ringing of the bell kept getting louder until a man and his donkey came into view. It was hard to make out just who it was, but Gray prayed in his own way that it was the prospector. He wanted to get some sleep, not another confrontation.

"Hi, folks," he said as he pulled on the donkey's rope. "Penny smelled your smoke, and wanted me to check it out. You know grass fires around here happen about this time of the year."

Gray jumped up. "Elias. It's you, and Penny. I am Gray, and this is Joe. The man you saved in the desert last year." Gray waited. "Remember us?"

The old man scratched his head. "Oh, Yeah, I do now. I think my mind is slipping a little. What are you doing out here in this part of the country, anyway?"

Elias released the rope, and Penny walked over to the fire. She sniffed around it for a minute, and then gave out a heehaw. Joe and Gray looked at Penny.

"Don't worry about that. She must smell the food you had."
"And the bear too!" Gray added.

"A grizzly bear, was it?"

"Yeah, we had one come by," Joe casually said. "Tell me more." Elias was interested.

"It's been an interesting night so far. A big grizzly, in fact, the biggest I have ever seen, came charging into our area, but it stopped at our fire. It sniffed the embers, so I threw it a piece of our meat. It grabbed the meat, and ran off back into the trees over there," Joe said as he pointed in that direction.

Elias smiled. "Oh, that sounds like Toby's pet bear. He raised it from a cub. He named it Grover after one of the presidents of our United States of America."

"You do mean Grover Cleveland? He's our president now. Joe remarked.

"And our territory will be an official state soon." Elias rejoiced.

Gray spoke up. "So you were right, Joe. Grover is somebody's pet, but a scary one at that."

Elias sensed Gray's concern. "Don't you worry, my friend? Grover would not hurt anyone. I've played with him for a few years now, and he only bit me once."

"Bit you once?" Gray exclaimed. "Where?"

"He was a young cub, and wanted something in my saddlebag. I tried to stop him. He didn't like it, so he bit me hard on my arm."

Elias pulled the end of his sleeve up his right arm. "You see those two big scars right below my elbow?"

Gray had a hard time seeing them, so Elias turned into the moonlight.

"I see them now. They're big, and bad looking."

"Grover broke both bones. Toby reset them as best as he could.

The arm still works."

He is a grown bear who has become a big loveable pet for Toby.

Grover is his bodyguard, you might say."

A moment of silence prevailed before Elias spoke again.

"I was on my way to meet up with Toby. It's a ways back in those trees. Would you like to come along? Toby loves company. He can tell you the names of our presidents and their families."

Joe was unsure. "I don't know, Elias. We want to get an early start in the morning. I want to get to Soledad City. I have to catch a couple of bad criminals, and bring them back to Bitter Wells for trial."

"Well, you do what you have to, but Toby always has a good pot of beans on the fire. I bet he is waiting for me, right now."

"I don't know." Joe looked at Gray. "What do you say? Do you want to go with Elias to see Toby's camp, and get some beans?"

"Why not go? We are not getting any sleep here. And I would like to try his beans, and maybe pet the bear."

Joe looked at Elias. "We're going."

Joe turned to face Gray and issued a command. "Get our horses ready now."

A tiny, winding path led them to a small clearing. Toby, an old crippled man dressed in a worn out military suit, was stirring the pot of beans. Grover was sitting on his haunches beside a chair made from tree limbs. A small musical instrument of some kind was leaning against one of the chair legs. His shelter was a piece of canvas draped over a tree branch, and pegged to the ground. Some tin cans and litter were scattered around.

Gray tied the horses' reins to a tree branch.

"Howdy, Elias. Glad you could make it. I see you brought some friends along."

"Yeah, this is Joe Lundy. Remember I told you about him last spring?"

Toby just nodded.

"And this is Gray who really saved Joe's life out there in the damn dry basin. He did a good job, I might add."

Toby looked up, and reached out, to shake Joe and Gray's hands. "Anybody that's a friend of Elias is a friend of mine. Welcome to you both."

"Thanks Toby. Looks like you have a nice little setup for yourself. Is this where you live? Joe questioned.

"No, I follow the seasons with Grover, my big old grizzly. He likes the snow in the winter, and, usually, takes a three-month nap while I do some trapping. Then, I go into the nearest town for supplies, and camp out beside Grover's den."

Gray had to ask. "Mister, can I pet Grover?"

"You sure can, just don't touch his ears. He will nip at you, and you all bleed. There is a leather ball I made inside my tent. Get it, and play fletch with him."

Gray walked to the tent. Grover gave him a long stare. Then, the bear got up off his haunches, and became excited when he saw Gray roll the ball toward him.

"Elias, grab a bowl, and have some of my delicious beans." "I think I will just do that."

"Joe, grab yourself a bowl of hot beans too." "It smells real good. I think I will."

Toby walked over to his chair, plopped down, and reached in his coat pocket for his pipe and tobacco. While he readied his pipe for a smoke, he asked Joe why he was in these parts.

First, Joe tasted the beans, "The beans have a good flavor. I'm interested in how you made them."

"I mix three kinds of beans with black strap molasses, ginger, onions, tomatoes, a dash of hot pepper. Then, I simmer that baby for hours over a fire of mesquite logs."

Joe swallowed another spoonful.

"We are on our way to Soledad City to arrest a couple of

outlaws." He pulled his badge out of his pants pocket, and showed to Toby "I am a deputy from Bitter Wells. I intend to bring them back to our town for a trial."

Toby noticed Joe's peg leg. "Sounds like a big job for you and the boy."

Elias interrupted. "I have known Joe for a very short time, but I can tell he's a strong, determined man. He'll get those outlaws. You just wait and see."

"Thanks Elias for the good words. I try to do my best. That's all anyone can do."

Gray was half listening to the conversation. "Yeah, Joe is my leader."

Toby looked at Gray, smiled, and then turned his attention to Elias. "Why are you here this time of the year? I don't see you until the leaves have fallen."

Elias reached inside the bag on Penny's back and pulled out a tied up rag. He opened it, and shown everyone what he had.

"You see this? I washed it in a stream but some of Penny's poop still remains on it."

Everyone stared at the item, and they were not sure what it was.

Elias moved closer to the fire, so everyone could get a better look. "Penny and I were searching a stream bed a while ago. Penny had

to poop. She dropped her pile of crap right on the edge of the water. As the water washed the poop downstream, I noticed something shiny and sitting on the bottom. I picked it up, and said, "Eureka." It was a gold nugget, one that was bigger than the one I already have."

Elias rolled it around in the rag. "See its gold color." Elias's face lit up every time he saw the nugget. "I've been searching most of my life for another gold nugget when Penny finds this one, and hers is even bigger."

Both Joe and Toby were amazed at its size.

"So what are you going to do with it? Save it for another twenty years?" Toby asked.

"No, I am on my way to Soledad City too. I want to see what it's worth. Maybe, I will quit prospecting, and go live in a big, fancy hotel in San Francisco."

Joe mentioned. "I'm glad you found it. It's been a long time. But why are you going to Soledad City? The best people for assaying gold, and telling you what it is really worth in Miner's Creek."

Elias replied, "It used to be that way, but the town is now being taken over by some corrupt businessmen. The man that I trust has moved to Soledad City. I know he will tell me what it is really worth."

"Well, Elias, why don't you and Penny travel to Soledad City with us tomorrow morning?" Joe asked.

"Penny and I are slow walkers. You must want to get to Soledad as soon as possible to catch those criminals."

"Yeah, that's true. But I would prefer to keep you company. The criminals can wait a little while longer."

Elias nodded as he walked over to Penny, and started to pull a blanket out of a leather bag.

Joe looked at Gray and Grover. They look like they are pals. Toby was smiling.

"Gray, get our bedrolls off the horses. It's time to hit the hay." Gray looked at Joe, and then at Grover.

"You can say goodbye to Grover in the morning. Rest time is now," Joe said, with firmness in his voice.

Gray was hearing that word "now" again, so he quickly set up the bedrolls.

Toby lifted the pot of beans off the fire, carried it inside his shelter, and placed it on the soft ground next to his bed of branches. He knew the warmth of the glowing embers would cancel out the coolness of the night, at least, for a while. Grover would hunker down next to the shelter, after it had made its trip into the woods to take a piss break.

After feeding his donkey a carrot, Elias was starting to set up a place for Penny and him to rest, while Gray and Joe were about ready to bed down.

"Gray, help me get this peg leg off me." "Is it bothering you?"

"Yes, it is starting to itch again. I have some of that stuff Amy used on me. It's in my saddlebag."

Gray unbuckled the straps, and pulled the peg leg off. In the dim light, he could see some redness over a good portion of the stump. It was smelly and sweaty as well.

Gray pulled a small jar of ointment out of the saddlebag, and hurried back to Joe. He rubbed the ointment over the redness. He also took a look at the end of the stump.

"How does it look?"

"Except for the redness, the stump looks good." "What about the end of the stump?"

"The end of the stump is good too."

"Then, put the peg leg on my bed roll next to my gun and holster. I'll sleep without it."

Gray did as he was told, and then started to lie down on his bedroll. Sleep was about to come to Joe and Gray, when they heard a slight rustle of a few tree leaves, then a soft movement of a footstep on soft ground. Instinctively, both of them knew it was the sounds of one or two men, and they knew also that they were not Indians. These men were too noisy. Joe started to reach for his gun, but it was too late.

Emerging into the clearing were two young men leading two very sweaty, brown horses. Joe could see the horses were worn out. The two men stopped in the center of the clearing, firing their guns in the air, and demanding an answer to a question.

"Okay, which one of you is Elias?" There was no answer, at first.

"Okay, I'll ask one more time, but I won't ask a third time. If no one answers up, then I will be sending all of you straight to heaven or hell."

Elias stepped forward. "I am Elias. What do you want?"

We live on the ranch where you and that jackass of yours were walking. One of our ranch hands saw you pick something up out of the creek. I think you had found some gold. We want it now. It belongs to us." The leader pointed his gun at Elias's nose. He was dead serious, and Elias knew it.

Elias put his hand on Penny's neck. This is a donkey, I remind you, not a jackass."

The other man pointed his gun at the donkey. He yelled. "Give us all your gold, or I'll shoot that damn donkey."

Elias hesitated.

The man fired one shot at the donkey, hitting it on the front leg.

Penny heehawed, and started kicking her leg, trying to get rid of the pain.

"Stop the damn shooting. I'll tell you all you need to know."

Elias began to explain the situation. "Penny and I were crossing your ranch lands, walking along Cedar Creek. We stopped once, and I noticed she had been eating some wild berries that grew near the water. I told her it was not good for her to eat them. She can be stubborn. She walked over to the creek, and dropped a load of crap right in the water. The water was flowing pretty well at the time. I looked down, and saw something glittering on the bottom. I reached down at the edge of the creek, and picked it up. I rolled it around in my hands, removing much of Penny's crap. I realized it was a gold nugget, a big one, at that."

Out of the corner of his eye, the leader saw Joe inch closer to a holster, and trying to pull a gun out of the holster. The leader turned, and fired a few shots at Joe's gun. The bullets ricocheted off the gun handle, but hurt no one.

"Get your hand away from that gun, and kick it over here."

The leader became amazed. "My, oh my, I see you have just one leg. Isn't that a shame? Did you lose it in the Civil War, or did some Indian cut it off for a coup? And what the hell are you doing out here on one leg, anyway?" He thought for a second. "Maybe, you can't kick the gun over here, after all."

He looked at his partner, and in a demanding voice, he said, "Luis, you taught Diablo how to kick a ball, so take your horse over there, and have him try to kick the gun over here. If he ruins it, who cares?"

"Si. I can do that."

That was all that Joe needed. He saw his chance.

As Luis led the horse toward the gun and holster, it temporarily blocked the leader's view.

Joe went into a squatting position, jumped up on his good leg, and dove for his gun. With complete accuracy, he shot the man leading the horse, and hit the other man while firing from beneath the belly of the horse. The horse jumped in fear, and ran away into the woods. Both men were shot in the hip, and screaming bloody murder. Both men had dropped their weapons.

Gray stood up fast, picked up the leader's gun, and pointed it at both of them. Joe stood up on one leg, and hopped over the leader, who was groaning in severe pain.

"You and your partner. I know you. You live on the Santo ranch. Both of you are good shooters. I've hunted with you. I'm a deputy now, and I have to bring both of you to Soledad City for trial. Why did you make this stupid attempt at robbery? The law states, very clearly, the creek is open property to all. It doesn't belong to you, or anybody else. What Elias found in the creek is his, and only his."

Joe could see Toby was standing outside his shelter. He looked the leader in the eye. "This is for my peg leg, and that donkey you shot."

Joe reached back, and threw a haymaker that landed on the leader's jaw. Joe twisted around on his leg, and fell down, but watched the leader stumbling backward, into the shelter, and then heard a kind of a plop sound. He had landed in the pot of beans.

Toby looked inside, and laughed. "It looks like he likes my beans. Most people put them in their mouth. This guy has to be different, I guess."

"Get him out of there before he has blisters all over his ass. He has to walk to Soledad tomorrow morning," Joe said.

Toby rolled the leader off the pot, and onto the dirt floor. Toby was an old codger who had big biceps. He grabbed both arms of the leader dragging him outside. Everyone could see the leader's Levis were burnt bad with beans smashed in them. He cut a piece of rope off his lasso, and tied the leader's hands behind his back.

Toby was tired from all the excitement, so he sat down in his chair, and started playing an Irish lullaby on his homemade ukulele.

Gray and Elias tie the other man to a tree. "Let him think about what he did. In the morning, we'll take him into town. A good walk will do both of them good."

Gray interrupted Toby as he began to sing. "Toby, do you have something to take care of Penny's leg?"

"Yes, I used to have a donkey, myself, years ago. I kept a lot of her medicine and supplies."

Toby picked up a bag from inside the shelter, looked at the leader still facedown, and moved fast to Elias and Penny. There, he checked out Penny's leg.

"After my examination, I can find no broken bones, just a small chip out of one, and a hole in the skin. I'll put some honey on her leg, and wrap a piece of a rag around the area. The wound should heal in a day or two."

Toby looked up at Joe who was now teetering on one leg. "We'll be safe tonight. Grover is about to come back. He will stand guard all night. Nothing moves on his watch."

"I knew I liked Grover for some reason. You have a good watchdog.

I mean good watch bear," said Joe.

Toby smiled and Gray agreed.

"Gray, let's try again to get a nap in before the sun rises." "Okay."

While everyone slept, Toby continued to play his lullabies.

Chapter

18

Toby awoke to Grover's low grumble. The bear was hungry. Toby did a quick check on the two prisoners, and then hurried to get a fire going. He put some bacon pieces and eggs he had scrambled into a large cast iron frying pan. Then, he broke a loaf of stale bread into pieces, and mixed it in. The coffee pot was always kept full of water, so Toby dumped in a half cup of coffee grounds, and placed it on part of the fire. This was Grover's favorite breakfast.

Grover grumbled a little louder. The bear seemed to be saying, "Hurry up."

Toby walked over, and gently patted Grover's head. "The eggs are getting done, ol' fella. Breakfast will be ready soon. I know you're hungry." He spoke softly.

But Grover seemed to pay no attention. This time, he let out a loud roar that seemed to vibrate off the surrounding trees.

Like an alarm clock, it awoke the rest of the camp. It was early morning, and just a few rays of light were filtering through the tree branches.

"Sorry for Grover's roar. He's really hungry." Toby apologized aloud.

Gray hurried to help Joe put his peg leg on, to roll up both bedrolls, and to have the horses ready for the day's journey. He walked them down the path to a grassy area, where they could have their breakfast of wild oats and grass. The prisoners' horses were nowhere to be found.

Nature was calling, so Gray stepped behind a nearby tree to urinate, and then headed to the stream. There, he wetted his face and hands, and dried them on his loincloth.

When he returned to Toby's camp, he saw the two prisoners were still tied to a tree, begging for something to eat. Elias, and Toby were sitting on their bedrolls, a tin plate full of eggs resting on their laps, and their right hands holding mugs of hot coffee. Joe was sitting on the end of a fallen tree trunk, trying to eat his breakfast. Using his left hand, he alternated from the tin plate to the mug of black coffee.

Toby saw Gray coming, and said, "Have some breakfast before Grover takes it all."

"Thanks Toby, I think I will join you."

As Gray scooped out some of eggs, one of the prisoners shouted. "You, asses, you will feed a savage, but not us. We've been telling you we're hungry too."

Joe became quite mad. "That savage is my partner. He saved my life. Be careful what you say."

From then on, the two prisoners knew they had to remain quiet throughout the rest of the breakfast.

Joe calmed his temper. Now, he felt a sense of obligation flooded his soul. He reached in his saddlebag, pulled out the remaining half of beef jerky, and threw it at the feet of the prisoners.

"How are we going to eat it? We can't reach it," they moaned.

Joe swallowed a mouthful of coffee, and then spoke. "You'll get to eat it soon enough As everyone began breaking camp, the prisoners proclaimed. "You've finished your breakfast. Now, please untie us from this damn tree, so we can eat."

Joe looked at Toby who was taking down his shelter, then at Elias and Gray. "Okay, it's about time to move on."

Joe stood up, and pulled his gun out of its holster. "Gray, cut the ropes that are holding them to the tree, but not the ones around their wrists."

Everyone waited, and watched the prisoners' teeth tear off chunks of jerky, and swallow it like ravenous some wolves.

"Why are all of you watching us? Maybe, if you had fed us last night, we wouldn't be so damn hungry," the leader said.

"Don't you get fed at home?" Toby retorted as he finished

packing his belongings.

"Not all the time. Papa gets the lion's share first."

Joe, with his gun in his hand, walked over to face them.

"Both of you should know better. You and your papa have a large ranch. Elias has only his donkey. You should have left him alone, but now you are facing a fine or jail time. We're heading back the way we came through these woods, and back on the main road to Soledad City. I want no problems. Understand? Both of you walk in front of Gray and me."

Both of them nodded as Joe looked back at the empty camp, and a dead fire pit.

"Toby, don't you need a horse?" Joe asked.

"No, thanks, but I have everything on an old Alaskan sled I bought. Sometimes Grover will pull it, but most of the time I wind up doing it." "Thanks for the beans, and eggs," Joe said. "Be careful. The sheriff in Bitter Wells said a stagecoach was robbed coming out of Soledad City last year, and the robbers have never been caught."

"Thanks for the advice, Toby said, but Grover and me are going in a different direction."

Joe turned his attention to the man adjusting the reins on Penny. "Elias, are you coming with us? You'll be safer if we are alltogether.

Could be bandits ahead of us," Joe cautioned.

"Yes, Penny and I are ready to follow you. I want to find what my gold is worth."

"Good. Let's get a move on."

Joe, Gray and Elias led their animals back through the twisty trail, over the stream, and onto the road that led to Soledad City.

The sun's heat was getting stronger, but a soft breeze tempered the feel of it.

After an hour following the dusty road, Gray spots two horses in an open field. He rode closer to Joe, and whispered.

"Joe, do you see the two horses in the field on my side?"

"Yes, they are following us. I believe they are our prisoners' horses."

"What should we do?"

"Nothing right now. Those horses are nervous, and they have a right to be. See how long they follow us? A Pawnee brave once told me if you push a mustang too hard, it will distrust you, and might never get over it. Those horses haven't reached that point yet."

The two horses kept pace with the men, but always at a safe distance. They would stop, eat some weeds, look in Joe's direction, and then move along at the same pace.

Finally, Joe needed an answer. Patience, it seems, was not always his strongest suit.

Joe turned Rain to face the horses. Rain saw them, shook his head, and gave a strong whinny.

Joe looked down at the prisoners.

"Hey you, the leader. I know your last name is Santos. Tell me. What do people call you?"

The leader started to walk, and didn't look back.

"I'll ask you one more time. Either cooperate with me, or face a big jail term. I can arrange that."

The leader stopped, did not look back, but spoke. "My name is Julio, and my brother is Dan."

"You do speak some English?" Joe was pleased. "Si, gringo."

"Dan? How did your brother get that name?"

"My father is a Mexican. His second wife is a Yankee. She named him."

"Good. Now we are getting somewhere."

"Did you see the two horses in the field on my left side?" Both Julio and Dan nodded a little. "We see them."

"Do they belong to both of you?"

There was a pause as both prisoners stared out into the field.

Dan spoke up. "I think the brown one with a black saddle is my horse."

Julio spoke next. "I am not sure. The horses we rode here belong to our father. We just took the first ones we could get a saddle on."

Joe looked at Gray.

"Well, if we keep going at this pace, it will be dark by the time we get to Soledad City. I want to get there before sundown."

"What do you want to do?" Gray wondered. Joe was about to put his plan into action.

He looked at the man holding the reins of his donkey.

"Elias. I want you to keep going forward. Don't stop. The rest of us will stay back for a while. We'll catch up to you a little later."

Elias seemed to know what Joe had up his sleeve as he passed by everyone. "See you all later."

Joe dismounted, and pointed Rain's nose to the two horses. He whispered an order in his horse's ear. "Go get them, Rain. Tell them we mean no harm." Then, he slapped Rain on his rump, and watched him race across the open field, straight to the two surprised horses.

Everyone watched as the three horses jockeyed for position and leadership. A little tussling, and nipping occurred, but it soon became clear who was in charge. Joe yelled a command, and Rain led the two horses straight to Joe and Gray.

Joe grabbed the reins of one horse, while Gray grabbed the reins of the other one. They walked them to Julio and Dan.

"I don't care which one of the horses you take. Just climb aboard, and take good care of them. Both of you stay right in front of me. Understand?"

Julio and Dan showed acceptance of his word, and climbed aboard. Everyone started moving forward once again. In a while, they had caught up with Elias. He looked at the new horses, and the men riding them. Then, he gave Joe a wink. Both knew Penny would never get along with rider less horses.

The sun had moved across the azure sky and was partly hidden by a patch of clouds as the four men began to travel a road that was going uphill. Joe stopped everyone when they came to a big bend in the road. They had just passed a rocky outcrop and were about to head downhill into a secluded valley. Soledad City lay just ahead.

Gray with his excellent eyesight was the first one to spot a covered wagon halfway down the hill. There were people in funny outfits fighting a man riding a horse.

He pointed to it, and spoke to Joe. "I see a lot of strange people running around a covered wagon. Do you see them?"

"Not as good as you can, but I do see something. Let's go slowly so we can get a closer look."

Joe nudged Rain forward, pushing Julio's horse. "Stay close together. There is something happening down below. Elias, you stay in back of us."

Everyone moved very cautiously, trying not to make any noises. As they got closer, it became clearer what was happening. A covered wagon with pots and pans hanging on its sides was stopped in the middle of the road. Two men and, maybe, twenty women were screaming, while trying to pull two people off a horse.

"Who are those strange looking people?" Gray asked in amazement. "And who is that guy on the horse?"

"They are Chinese. They came to this country to help build the big railroad that goes from the west coast of this land to the east coast of this land. They worked like slaves blasting tunnels through Sierra Mountains. Now that the railroads are completed, they are no longer needed. If they don't go back to China, they must find new work here." Joe could sense a growing unrest, and realized he had to do something fast to stop it. He also knew his badge was not enough, and his weapons were not enough either.

He asked the two prisoners to turn around. "There is big trouble down there in that wagon train. I need your help. If you will ride in there with Gray and I, firing our guns in the air, we should be able to stop it."

"I will make a deal. If you do what I ask, I will forget your crimes, and you can go home free men. Are you with me?"

"We are." Their vote was unanimous.

"Good. Gray cut their ropes, and give them back their guns." Gray did as ordered.

Julio and Dan seemed pleased. Julio quickly checked the ammunition in his gun, and smiled. "Let's go."

Joe and Gray led the charge down the hill, firing their guns in the air, and into the middle of the people. The people looked up at the approaching party. They became scared, and started dropping their weapons: some of which was rakes and shovels.

Things settled down quickly. Joe told Gray to take over while he rode over to the man and young woman sitting on a big brown horse. He was dressed in some kind of military uniform with some blood trickling down his forehead. He was holding an old buffalo rifle in one hand, and a fearful Chinese girl in the other.

"Howdy. My name is Joe Lundy. I am a deputy in these parts. "I see you are a buffalo soldier."

"Yeah, that's me. My name is Nat Scott. I'm a soldier with the Seventh Calvary."

"I'm surprised to see you in this area. Most of the fighting is down south of here with the Apaches."

"That's right. I got myself tied up with this young lady in Soledad City. We got hitched there. Her name is Jia Far (beautiful flower), and these barbarians are trying to keep her from moving away with me. It's a damn shame. They kept yelling nigger, nigger to me, and whore to Jia Far. I can take it, but I know she cannot.”

“So what happened and why here?”

“We rode up to the wagon to say goodbye. They stopped, and we had some tea. Everything was fine, until I tried to leave here with my lady. These people wouldn’t let me. See that big bastard in the shorts. I didn’t see him coming, and he tried to kill me by swinging his arm like it was a sword. He hit my shoulder. It hurt like hell, but both of us made it to my horse, and we were trying desperately to leave.”

Joe turned attention to Jia Far. “Do you speak any English?” “A little,” she said.

“I speak some too,” Nat offered. “I want to hear Jia speak.”

“Do you want to be with this man? Do you want to go with him today?”

“Yes.”

Joe pointed to all the people standing. “Do you want to leave all your friends?”

“Yes.”

“My parents are dead. I am Cantonese.” “Those people are from Hunan,” Nat added.

Joe looked into Jia’s eyes. He had never seen such beautiful eyes. “Tell me more.”

“They do not treat me well. I want to be free like you. Let me go.” “Thanks Jia. Would you and Nat please tell these people what I am about to say?” “Yes.”

“Yes.”

Joe turned to the crowd, and pointed to the couple on the horse. “These people are free to go. Don’t try to stop them, or I will have to shoot you. You are free. Let these two people go free too.” Joe shook Nat’s hand. Both of you go in peace.”

Joe rode to Julio and Dan. “Thanks for your help. You are free to go. Maybe we can do some hunting when I get back to Bitter

Wells."

"Since, we are not too far from Soledad City, we'd like to stay there over one night before we head home, and then we'll have a long talk with our father," Julio said.

"Take care of your horses, and keep your noses clean in that town. I hear the sheriff is hard on people who break the law, and I can't bail you out, either. We are going to camp at the bottom of this hill. I know there's good grass and water for the horses and donkey. We'll get an early start in the morning."

As Julio and Dan turned their horses toward town, both saw Elias feeding Penny some oats. Dan smiled, and tipped his hat. "Enjoy the gold. He said.

Chapter
19

Soledad City was a prosperous, little town nestled among some rolling hills, somewhat hidden from the migrants that were traveling west to California. It had two main streets that intersected at an elaborate water fountain in the town square. The fountain had been erected in honor of Jose Garcia Sanchez, a Mexican farmer and part time explorer. Jose would often tell people he was a descendant of the Spanish explorer Hernando De Soto, and possessed the same urge to wander the southwest.

It was during an April rain that Jose discovered a spring of pure, salt free water. It tasted so good that he decided it would make a good home for his family and relatives. The settlement grew into a town. Jose named it after his birthplace. The townspeople built the fountain, and named it, "Tlatoc," an Aztec rain god, in his honor.

Clean looking adobe homes and shops painted in different colors lined both streets. Women dressed in colorful dresses and holding parasols were admiring gold and turquoise necklaces that a shop owner had on display. A group of children were playing a game of tag in the street, and a few men were walking up and down the streets hawking their wares. The smell of fresh baked bread permeated the air as Joe and Gray rode into town. Elias had already stopped at the assayer's office.

It was noontime as they hitched their horses to the post outside the sheriff's office. As Gray dismounted he couldn't help to marvel at the tall building at the end of the street. He remembered Joe had told him he had traveled to this town once before, so Gray knew he would have an answer. "Joe, what is that big building?"

"That building is the capital, the judge's quarters when he is in town, the town jail, and, of course, the town saloon or as the people around here like to call it "The Mariposa" or butterfly to you. The building is made of solid wood planks from an Old Spanish galleon that Jose and his family brought here many years ago.

The building is the only place in the territory where you can be arrested, tried, sentenced, and put in prison, all in the same day. Don't go in it, I warn you."

"Is Jose still alive?"

"No, he died about ten years ago."

"Yeah, many moons ago." Gray was trying to poke a little fun at him. He knew only too well what Joe was saying.

Joe and Gray walked into the sheriff's office. Everything inside caught Gray's attention. The place was immaculate. He did not see a crumb or cigar ash anywhere on the polished oak floor. He couldn't believe the cleanliness, not even his tepee with Spotted Feather's help was ever this clean. He briefly glanced at the artwork on the walls as Joe and he continued to walk toward a small jail cell at the back of the office. The sheriff was talking to a young man behind bars.

"Fernando, I had to lock you up. You do know why?" the sheriff asked.

"I guess so. I'm not supposed to lift up a girl's dress." "That's right." The sheriff retorted.

"But all I wanted to see was her beautiful legs. My pals claimed they did it."

"I don't care what your pals saw. You were caught by the teacher." "I'm sorry." Todd sank back onto the cot, his hands holding his head.

"I understand. I was a kid once." The sheriff tried to show a little sympathy.

"Well, the girl's parents filed a complaint. The sheriff added. You're not old enough to stay in the "Mariposa" jail, so you'll have to stay here."

"When can I get out of here?"

"You'll have wait for the judge to see you in a day or two."

"Day or two?" the young man yelled. "I have to help my father mend some fences, or he'll tan my ass."

"Watch your language."

The sheriff turned around when he sensed somebody was behind him. "What can I do for you?"

"Howdy, sheriff. My name is Joe Lundy. I am a deputy in Bitter Wells, and this is my partner, Gray." "I see your badge."

The sheriff stared at Gray. "You have a young Indian for a friend?" The sheriff was mystified.

"Yes. He's a good partner."

"Well, I guess that's okay. We have no Indians here, just mestizos, half-breeds like me. But I remind you we believe we are Americans, and do speak some English."

Jack reached out to shake Joe's hand.

"I am Jack Ortez, the sheriff in these parts."

Then, he walked back into his office. "A lovely town, isn't it? Nothing much happens around here. That's just the way I like it."

"Yes, it sure is. It's the best town around these parts. We in Bitter Wells hear nothing but good things coming out of here." Gray watched as Joe was trying to soften up the sheriff.

Sheriff Ortez sat down, and put some papers lying on the desk into a drawer. Then, he pulled out a stogie and began to light it up. He leaned back in his wooden chair and asked, "Bitter Wells is a good ways from here. What brings you out here? Whatever it is, it must be important."

"Sheriff."

"Call me Jack. We're both friends of the law." Jack took a big puff on the stogie. A ball of smoke filled the room, nearly choking Gray. The sheriff needed time. His mind was searching through the town's history. Why would this deputy travel so far to his town, and what help would he want? The answer was forthcoming, and the sheriff would not like it.

"Ten cows were slaughtered last winter on the Douglas ranch.

The ranch is ten miles south of Bitter Wells. The men who did this crime, put the cows in a circle, and took only the choicest cuts of meats. As a deputy, I was asked to find these men, and bring them back to Bitter Wells for trial."

"Why a circle?" Jack was curious. "We don't know."

"You mean to say you are here looking for two men who killed ten cows?"

Joe nodded. "Last winter?"

"Don't you think their trail is cold by now? And why, of all places, would they come here?"

"First, I had to get the buildings on the Douglas ranch in better shape. We had a bad winter. A lot of repairs had to be made."

"Second, I spent years as a scout for the U.S. army. Tracking down people is my business. I know these men are here."

"And how do you know that, may I ask?" Jack was getting a little huffy, and Joe could see it.

"Did you see their footprints in our street?" the sheriff asked in a sarcastic tone.

Joe tried hard to control his temper. He took the opportunity to pull out of his pocket a homemade cigarette. He decided to take his time lighting it.

"Well. I'm waiting," Jack said, anxiously.

"No, no footprints. We went to a little town called Stampede. The sheriff had sent a telegraph stating he had the two men in his jail. Unfortunately, it wasn't them. It was a trick the real criminals played on us. They thought they were smart. But I figured they would come here to buy a wedding dress for a young woman that had decided to go along with them."

"So you think these men are here in my clean, respectable town, buying a wedding dress?"

"Yes, I do."

Sheriff Ortez paused, while he took another long puff. "And

who are these men? Do they have names?"

"Zach Reis and Jonas Diver. Very dangerous, I might add."

Jack reached down, and opened a second desk drawer Gray tried to push the cigar smoke aside, so he could move forward, and watch was about to happen.

Jack laid a crumbled pile of papers on his desk, and leafed through them. "I see no one with the names you gave me." A frustrated Jack Ortez stated.

"Are they wanted for anything else?" he said as he showed an unpleasant grin.

"Yes, Zach Reis was convicted for killing a butcher, but escaped from prison three years ago. He took the butcher's knife, and he likes to show it off by cleaning the food caught between his teeth. We have nothing on Jonas Diver."

Sheriff Ortez thought for a moment as he took another long puff, and then shook his head. Then he leaned forward, and looked straight into Joe's eyes.

"These men could have come into town yesterday while I was patrolling the other street."

"That seems right about the time they would have been here." Sheriff Jack leaned back once again in his chair.

"I must say you are one persistent man. You waited all this time. I hope you find them. But remember, I want no violence in my town. You arrest the men, and high tail it back to your town. That's the way I like it to be. Call me if you need any help. I'll be watching both of you."

Joe was silent. He turned and was about to walk toward the door. "There is a shop down at the end of this street that makes beautiful wedding dresses. You might want to check it out first." Jack stopped smiling, and took another long puff."

Once out of the office, they walked on a stone laid sidewalk, passing a few ladies along the way. Each one was courteous, and smiling.

"Joe, these stones we are walking on, fit so well together. It beats walking on creaky wooden boards or on mud when it rains." Gray stated.

"I was told these stones were hand carved by Aztec craftsmen a long time ago, and brought here. Jose wanted his town to be a beautiful place to live."

"I think he did it."

Joe and Gray came to a small adobe building near the end of the street. A gas lamp was attached to the wall, and a sign hung in the window saying "Senorita's Vestido." A wooden door was partly open.

Upon entering, they met a pretty middle-aged woman dressed in a colorful gown who greeted them with an enticing smile. Around her, there were wedding dresses hanging on rods attached to all the walls.

"Forasteros," she said boldly.

Joe and Gray were confused.

"Forasteros. Strangers, are you not?" she asked softly this time. Joe began to speak as Gray surveyed the inside.

Joe stressed their reason for being there. "Si, we are strangers. We are not here to buy a dress. We are here for information. Do you understand?"

"Si. No dress. Informacion? What do you want from me?" Joe could see the woman was acting uneasy. He had a limited knowledge of Spanish, but knew all kinds of sign language. Through hand moments and gestures, he knew he could get this woman to tell him what she knew.

"We want to know if two gringos came in here to buy a wedding dress for a young girl. Do you understand?

"Si. I understand now. "Two gringos came here yesterday with a girl. She looked scared and had a lump on her head. One man kept pointing his knife at me and at the girl. She picked a dress, but it needed some sewing. They should be here tomorrow morning. I tell you that man is loco. It's not my business to say anything, but that girl is in big trouble, I do believe."

"Gracias senora." Joe bowed slightly and kissed her left hand.

"No, amigo, I am a senorita." She smiled as she showed him her empty ring finger." She kept smiling. "You come back soon. We have some tequila. Watch the sunset. You bring your friend too. I have a little sister for him to meet."

Joe smiled and nodded, backed away, and then slipped out the doorway.

"That was close. She likes you a lot." Gray was pleased.

"I have no time for socializing. I'm here to arrest two criminals who broke the law. You can come back here to meet her sister, but not me." Joe was firm in his belief.

"No, you are my vision. I will follow you. Besides, I have a beautiful woman in Spotted Feather who is waiting for me."

"Good. You keep it that way."

Joe looked around. "We know they are somewhere in this town. Zach likes to gamble, so my guess is in the Mariposa."

Joe and Gray walked to the end of the street. Joe pulled out his revolver, and spun the barrel. He was satisfied, so he placed it back in the holster. He made sure the whip was on his right hip in case he might need it. He looked at Gray, and started to push the saloon doors open. Gray knew what he had to do. Stay outside, and be ready with his whip.

All the mestizos at the bar turned their heads and stared at the stranger. At once, one of them stood up and walked right up to Joe. He started picking between his teeth with his sharp bladed knife. "Hi Joe. "Just picking some Douglas beef from between my teeth." He swaggers his body a bit. "What brings you here?"

"You!"

Zach grinned. "I see someone made you a deputy. Gave up punching cows, I take it. Couldn't stand the smell of all that bullshit anymore?"

"I'd take bullshit any day over you."

"What do you want?" The man kept taunting Joe.

"I'm here only long enough to arrest you, Zach and your partner, Jonas, and bring both of you back to Bitter Wells. By the way, we have a nice jail cell waiting for you."

"Is it for killing ten cows that don't belong to you, or is it for your horse falling down a ravine with you on it?"

"I can't get you for killing my horse, and almost me, but the cows belonged to my boss."

"Oh, your boss. The one you like so much?"

Joe was deeply irritated. He started to reach for his gun.

"I wouldn't do that. My friend, Jonas, is at the other end of the bar, and he has his gun pointed at your head. Better back off, if you know what's good for you."

Joe relaxed his hand. He could see the odds were not in his favor. "Look around. These people are my amigos. I told them my mother was a Pawnee Indian. I am a mestizo like everyone here.

"Your mother was no Indian. She was the butcher's wife, a white woman. You killed your father."

Joe could see all the people with stubborn faces knew little English and were starting to come toward him.

"I'll be back."

"I am counting on it." Zach waved his right hand. "See, my right hand and my right leg works!" Zach laughed.

Joe turned, walked through the saloon doors, and straight to the sheriff's office. He knew he needed the sheriff's help to avoid a shoot- out.

Zach turned to face the rest the crowd of men. He had a grin that seems to go from ear to ear. He twirled his knife in the air, and let the point dig into the bar. His plan was working.

A very frightened girl lay huddled in the back corner of the Mariposa.

Chapter
20

The sheriff could see real concern on Joe's face as he and Gray stepped into his office. Jack was worried. Earlier, a bystander had rushed into his office, and warned him there was a lot of tension developing in the Mariposa. Since his town was such a peaceful place harboring no known criminals, Jack had hoped a capable deputy like Joe would have an easy time arresting the two men he was after, and then quickly skedaddled out of town. He was also worried that the tension would grow into a dangerous situation. He did not want any townsfolk getting killed, or even hurt.

"Jack, we need your help. Zach told the others in the Mariposa that he was a mestizo just like them, and they believed him. The mestizos seem to speak little English, They would listen to Jonas who repeated the words that Zach had spoken." A thought occurred to Joe. "Jack, I do remember when we were herding the cattle at night; Jonas would sing Mexican songs to them. He said it made the cows relax."

Sheriff Jack Ortez stood up, opened a drawer, and lifted a huge revolver out of it. Gray could not imagine a handgun being that big. He thought must have weighed a lot because the sheriff's wrist twisted downward, at first. Then, with two arms, he raised it up, and pointed it toward the ceiling.

"This is my weapon. It roars like a Mexican cannon. It's a scary thing. When it fires, I can't hear for a week. You better put something in your ears."

Joe wasn't convinced. "It might do the trick, but I think we need more men. A posse would do."

"That'll never happen. I don't even have a deputy. The people around here have been free from crime for so long, that they think they don't need a posse either. Last year, the town council was considering whether my job was really needed. Imagine a town without a lawman?"

Joe looked at Gray. "Are you ready to fight those bad men that I am after? You'll have a lot to lose."

"My place is with you until I find a Great Gray Owl feather. Then, my vision is complete, and I can return to my people. Whatever you want to do, I am with you."

"Thanks, Gray. I appreciate that. You're a brave, young man." "Now, take your bandana, tear four small strips of material out of it,

spit on each one, and then, roll it up into a ball." Gray did not ask why. Joe continued. "Give me two of them. Push them into your ears like I am doing. It's to keep out the noise."

Joe turned back to the sheriff. "Let's do it. Maybe the metizos will listen to you, or to that big gun of yours."

Jack walked around the desk, and led them outside. As they began to head down the street, two men riding horses and a man pulling a donkey caught up to them. It was Julio, Dan, and Elias.

"The town is buzzing. We hear there is going to be some gunfire in the Mariposa. They say two men have aroused a group of mestizos to fight with them. Is this true?" Julio asked.

"Yes, it's true. We are headed there right now. Want to join us?" Joe asked.

"We wouldn't miss the chance." Dan agreed.

Julio and Dan tied the reins of their horses to a hitching post.

Joe looked at a quiet Elias. "How did you do at the assayer's office?"

A happy Elias did a little jig.

"I hit it big. I could go to San Francisco, and live like our president. But then, I thought of Penny, and what would happen to her. I looked inside the moneybag I was holding. It was no decision. My life is here with my best friend, Penny. As I came out of the assayer's office, I couldn't decide what to do with the bag of money. That problem was quickly taken care of. Julio and Dan came riding by. I waved, and yelled to them. "Come over here. I want to talk to you." I reached in my bag and gave them half of the money. I felt it was theirs as much as it was mine."

"I agree."

"Where are you headed to next?" Joe inquired.

"Joining up with you, that's where. I wouldn't miss the action. Then, Penny and I are headed toward the northwest. I heard gold was discovered in Alaska. A change of climate might do me some good."

"Let's keep moving!" a solemn Jack ordered.

Joe smiled to himself as the five men followed the sheriff to the Mariposa. He had his posse now.

The situation was about the same as before. Zach was at the bar drinking Tequila with Jonas, and a few mestizos. Zach looked up when he heard the saloon doors creak open.

He saw four men side by side, weapons drawn. Gray stayed outside.

First, Jack pointed his weapon at the crowd. When one mestizo sitting at a table saw the size of the barrel, he got up and hurried to the back of the room. Jack spoke Spanish in a strong, firm voice to the thirty or more mestizos. He told them, in no uncertain terms, Soledad City was a peaceable town for all mestizos. Jose Sanchez founded this town for people like them and their families." He asked, "Do you remember the ways you were treated in Juarez? How poor you were? How the rich Castillians looked down on you? Here, we are a free people, all as one. If you fight alongside of these two Yankees, you will destroy our town's reputation. Then, we will have many soldiers come here. We will lose our freedoms, and be poor people again. Do you want that, my amigos?"

Silence prevailed for a short time until Zach threw his glass across the room. "Don't listen to these so called lawmen. This is your town. They can't tell you what to do, can they?" Jonas repeated Zach's words in a loud Spanish voice.

The sheriff rebuked him in Spanish. "Zach is no mestizo. He lied to you. He is wanted for murder."

Joe spoke next. "I only want to take these two Yankees back to Bitter Wells for trial."

Jack repeated Joe's statement in Spanish.

When Zach saw he might be losing the argument, he reached down, and grabbed Alice by the hair. His sinewy arm picked up her frail body. He looked into her eyes, and then, threw her across the floor, like she was a rag doll.

"What about this whore? What are you going to do about her? Tell me, you big bad sheriff, and your tinhorn deputy."

The sheriff pointed the barrel of his weapon at Zach. He fired a huge bullet that whizzed past Zach's ear, and shattered several whiskey bottles on the wall behind the bar. The sound the gun made echoed throughout the Mariposa. Everyone's ears were ringing. All the mestizos were placing their hands over their ears, and crouching in pain.

"I've got more bullets." Jack announced. "Are you ready to listen?" "Okay, okay. Let's make a deal." Zach was shaking his head, while wielding his knife in the air.

"You have no deal!" Joe yelled back. "I am taking you and Jonas back to Bitter Wells. It's that simple."

"Okay, Joe. You want me, and I want you dead, lying on the ground out there in the street today."

Joe responded. "And how do you plan to do that? I think we are holding the aces. You, the deuces."

Jonas handed Zach a wet, red bandana. He rubbed his face and head.

Jonas yelled. "Sheriff, lower that cannon and listen to me. These mestizos still don't believe you, and we don't want any bloodshed around here, do we?"

Zach stated defiantly, "You can try to take my knife and my

gun from me. But I must warn you. I have my secret partner." He pointed to the side door." I paid him a heap of money to be here. All I have to do is give him the word, and he will knock all of you off like rusty beer bottles sitting on a fence."

"You're bluffing." Joe was getting irate. "You were always a loser at playing cards. You are a loser now!"

"Jonas, tell that mestizo next to you to open the side door."

As the door was opened, a tall, well-dressed man walked in. He stood next to Zach, and doffed his hat.

"Dallas Grat."

Joe was surprised. "What are you doing here? You said you always followed the money. This place doesn't have the kind of money you want."

"Well, a lot of money has led me here. You see Zach and Jonas robbed a stagecoach a few days ago. I figured I head up this way. Zach offered me all the gold in the strong box if I would come here, and shoot you. I am prepared for a gunfight outside in the street."

"A stagecoach?" Joe said.

Jack interrupted. "Yes, Joe, a stage out of a town north of here was robbed by two men wearing red bandanas."

Zach waved the damp red bandana Jonas had given him. "You can add that robbery to my sentence."

"Dallas, I thought you didn't like this little man whose height barely comes up to your belt buckle?" Joe questioned.

"Like I told you back in Bitter Wells, money is my friend. I also told you I would be seeing you again. That time is right now. Either go outside, or I will kill all of you right here in the Mariposa."

A happy Zach said, "I'll give the sheriff this little whore as a part of the deal."

Jack looked at Joe. "What do you say?

Joe thought for a second. He knew the town needed a good

sheriff, not a dead one, and he wanted to save Alice's life, so he agreed. Maybe Zach had an ace up his sleeve, but he didn't know Joe had one too.

Joe spoke directly to Dallas. "I have one condition for this gun fight. Both of us will have only one bullet in the chamber. One bullet. Since you were such a good shot at the match we had in Bitter Wells, you should need only one shot to take me down. Agree?"

"I agree. One shot will do it easily."

"I want the sheriff to check our guns first."

"Let's do it." Dallas snarled. "I want that bag of gold, so I can get out of town before sunset. And sheriff, if you try to stop me, you'll be resting next to Josiah. Oh, I forgot it's Joe." Dallas was trying hard to get Joe's goat. He knew a mad gunfighter is a careless one.

Zach walked over to Alice, and pushed her hard with his boot. When Dan began to pick her up, he could see she was bruised, and her eyes were swollen, but she still tried to smile. She would be happy to leave this town, and be going home.

All four men backed out through the saloon doors.

"Take the girl to my office. Get the woman that lives next door to help her." Jack ordered Dan.

Gray looked at Joe, a tired looking man. "Are you all right?"

"Yes, I am okay. I have one more thing to do, then we can be on our way home."

Joe took his gun, unlocked the cylinder, and dropped five bullets out of it. He showed the cylinder to the sheriff, who nodded. Joe made sure the lone bullet was in the firing chamber. Gray reached down and picked the bullets up and put them in his sacred rock bag.

"Joe, you are using only one bullet? A puzzled Gray asked. "Yes, Gray. That's all I will need."

Gray shook his head a little. White men are sometimes very

loco, he said to himself. He squeezed the rock bag, and prayed his leader knew what he was doing.

Joe proceeded to undo the belt holding his holster, and rotated it to the right hip He kept the belt loose, so the holster hung down, knee level. "How do I look?" Joe asked.

"I do not know. You didn't have it that way on the ranch, or at the shooting match in town. Why are you doing this now?"

"You'll see soon enough."

The sheriff wondered the same thing. Julio and Dan stood by, watching in silence.

Joe spoke to his partner. "Gray, see that man wearing a cowboy hat over there? The one with a gray feather in it."

"I see him."

"That might be a Great Gray Owl feather?"

"Have your whip ready. I can see he is a sneaky person, and he might try to ruin the gunfight."

"Yeah, sneaky. Like bad medicine." "Yeah, like bad medicine."

Sheriff Jack stared at Joe. "You don't have to do this. There are a few men working in the fields. I know they would help."

"It's too late for that."

Joe started walking to the center of the street; the holster was bouncing off his peg leg. Dallas was already there. He had the snap off his holster with the edge of his coat tucked behind him. He was an imposing figure like one you would find in a western dime store novel. His lips were taut, and his steely eyes were right below the brim of the hat. Golden hair could be seen flowing down his back, much like General George Custer. He was ready.

A sizeable crowd had gathered on both sides of the street. This impending gunfight was new to all the residents. Much like a hanging in Bitter Wells, these people were both curious and excited to see what was going to happen. To them, this was a big event, maybe, bigger than the yearly harvest celebration.

Joe walked to a specific spot, and faced Dallas, maybe, ten yards away. Joe didn't bother to check his gun. Both men were like living statues, ready to wage war.

Sheriff Jack stepped up to Dallas and checked his revolver. There was only one bullet in the cylinder. He walked to Joe, and checked his revolver too. Then he stepped back, and watched.

"Whenever you are ready, Dallas."

Joe made a faint move, bending over to get his gun.

Without hesitation, Dallas drew first. The bullet slammed into Joe's balsa leg. It made a jagged hole that went clear through.

Joe slowly raised his upper body, and pointed his gun at Dallas. "Drop your gun, and put out your right arm."

Dallas did as told. He spoke no words. Let me see your palm."

Dallas opened his palm, and waited.

Joe pointed his revolver in Dallas's direction, and fired his only shot. It went through Dallas's palm, shattering bone and tendons. Dallas did not flinch or yell out in pain. He simply looked at his palm in disbelief. His honor lost, he would have preferred death.

"Now, we have the same handicap, a useless right hand and trigger finger. I recommend you learn to use your left hand like I had to."

Joe started to turn and walk away when an enraged Zach standing on the side walk, drew his gun and aimed it at Joe.

"You son-of-a bitch, this time I'll do it myself."

Jack saw Zach, and fired his "cannon." In the mist of smoke and noise, the bullet found its mark. Zach fell backward. He laid flat on the ground. He uttered no words.

Next, Jonas attempted to do Joe in, but Gray had been watching him closely. Gray took his whip, and lashed out at Jonas's hand. The whip did its job. Gray could hear the bones crack. Jonas dropped his gun, and started screaming in pain. "You damn Indian. You bastard." He hollered for all to hear.

Julio and Dan grabbed Jonas, and started punching the crap out of him. Joe saw what was happening. He had to stop it. He walked over, and stood between them.

"Stop this now. I need this man alive, so I can take him back to Bitter Wells. We don't want a murder on our hands, do we?" He looked at the sheriff.

The sheriff nodded. "Take this man and throw him in my jail. I'll be there in a minute." He admired Joe for the way he handled the situation. He shook his hand. "Thanks. Our town thanks you too."

"Sheriff, don't forget to thank Gray. He saved my life twice." "Twice?" Jack turned to face Gray. Then, shook his hand. "Thanks, amigo."

Gray looked at both Joe and the sheriff. "Before they take Jonas away, I want to ask him a question."

Joe and the sheriff nodded.

"Jonas, I know you are in much pain, but tell me is that a Great Gray Owl's feather in your hat?"

"Why do you ask me such a stupid question when you see I am in pain. Get me a doctor."

"Well, is it?"

"Yes, it is. I took it off a dying Indian in Deadwood." Jonas shook in pain.

"That's all I wanted to hear." Gray pulled the feather out of Jonas's hat, and placed it in his hair next to the feather his uncle had given him.

As Jonas was escorted away, Gray yelled, "Thanks, Jonas. I'll take good care of it."

A young boy came forth, and gave Julio and Dan their horses. They said they were heading for home. With no fanfare, they mounted up. Julio looked down at Joe, tipped his hat, and said, "See you in the fall for a hunting trip?"

Joe nodded and waved goodbye as they galloped off. He

looked at Gray for the last time. Gray asked what he was going to do with Alice. He replied he would give Alice her wedding dress." He winked. "He might even decide to have Tequila with the store owner, and watch the sunset. In the morning he would take Alice back to her family in Stampede. Later he would come back for Jonas, and head for Bitter Wells.

Gray had one final question to ask. "Joe, how did you know Dallas would shoot you in your peg leg?"

"Remember, when Dallas and I were in the shooting match in Bitter Wells? He had a longer barrel put on his revolver for more accuracy, but that made the gun was unbalanced. When he started to fire, the barrel of the gun would drop just a little bit before he could raise it up. I figured if I bent over toward my right knee, he would shoot. Well, he did and you saw the results."

"That was amazing."

"Yeah, instead of having a notch on my gun handle, I now have a hole in my peg leg."

It was Gray's turn to say goodbye. "Joe, you have been a good leader, a good friend. With your help, I have completed my vision. I have my Great Gray Owl feather. I can go home. My uncle will be proud. So will Spotted Flower and the whole tribe. I have no more to say, except "Adios." I know that's not Nuchu, but it will do."

Another boy brought Gray his horse, already saddled. Gray climbed aboard, and gave the horse the command to get moving.

A very sad Joe waved for the last time, and said with a tear moving in his eye. "Adios to you, my son. I will miss you."

Epilogue

The lives of Joe Lundy and Gray Owl Waiting are like so many other people of their times. They have become lost between the pages of history. Good, common folk, young and old, some not as smart as others, some more humane, some more adventurous, all having a place in the settling of the American West. One knows all cannot be remembered for their experiences and deeds they had in their everyday living, but the end result speaks for itself. The West was settled, and America became the land of the free.

As for Gray Owl Waiting, he became a leader of his people, who taught them the ways of the white man and the consequences if they did not follow them. He saved his tribe and became a strong spokesman for Indian rights. He and Spotted Feather had two boys who became lawyers, and worked with the state government.

Joe Lundy was a different story. His trail appeared to head off into the sunset with little fanfare. What he did in his remaining life is questionable. He loved his partner, Gray, and sorely missed him when he returned to his tribe. Joe, however, would not stand in Gray's way to fulfill his vision and his goals. He cherished the love and support the Douglas Ranch gave him. He enjoyed being a deputy, and not being recognized as a fast gun, but a defender of the law and what the law stood for. So what happened to him?

Here's a possible hint. In a San Francisco newspaper, there was a baby announcement. It stated that Sarah Downing had given birth to a seven-and-half-pound boy, and she named him Joe.

Maybe, just maybe, the clouds do hold water for Joe Lundy, after all?

Peace brother.

The One-Legged Hesperian (cowboychart)

Chapter 1. Morning

Joe Lundy, cattle driver, falls down an arroyo, right hand useless, broken right leg.

Thunder, Joe's black 8-year-old horse, has broken leg, Joe shoots it, Canteen crushed, no water, he starts carrying prized saddle across

Utah's Wastach Basin, an arid place.

Uinta Mountain Range Saddle, has high arch.

Mesa, with two cottonwood trees

Cattle drive, **whip,** two prized bulls, **horns,** buffaloes scatter.

Crazy Dave's Saloon Delta D ranch

Zach, cattle driver, likes to pick his teeth with **knife, hates to lose** at **Poker,** is smaller than partner **Jonas,** Joe wins pot.

Chapter 2. Next Morning

Uinta Mountain Range

Whirligig, broken tree branch,

Joe gets **help.**

Joe Josiah Lundy, call him **Joe,** pencil **mustache,** thinning **hair,**

Fourteen-year-old Indian boy (call him Gray), baking **Indian bread** in an **old pot,** sending **smoke signals.**

Joe has **pain,** cannot move **right leg,**

Gray makes **splint,**

Uses **aloe** from **Yucca plant** for Joe's **face,**

Joe wants his **hat** and **locket, rifle** (no ammo), **silver saddle, Mayor, Santa Fe, palomino.**

Gray Owl Waiting, red paint on face, **hawk feather** in **black hair** with one **notch** meaning one **coup.**

Nuchu, (Northern Ute tribe).

Uncle Lone White Feather sends Gray to find his **vision, Great Spirit,**

Owns a **piebald horse** with **bell.**

White Flower, Gray wants to marry her.

Gray Owl feather, mother's wish, has great power.

His depressed parents froze to death.
Gray was sent back **East** to **Indian school,** learns **English.**
Gray's knife, has **spirit.**
Apache thieves,
Different **bell** sound,
Large **rock**, buffalo **water bag.**

Cowboy Facts

A western saddle weighs an average thirty pounds. They have better weight distribution and wider arch than an English saddle. Round items called Conchos were made of German silver and used as ornaments on the saddle. German silver has stainless steel in it and doesn't oxidize. German silver accent trim was sometimes used on the sides of the saddle.

Hereford cattle were first bred in Hereford, England, in 1817. Herefords were meatier and with small or no horns. They were introduced in the American West in 1882 to 1888. All became hornless and popular by 1890s.

Cowboy Life—What Was It Like?

1. In the sixteenth-century, Spanish settlers brought horses and cattle to New World.

2. Some of the horses and cattle were allowed to roam, freely grazing everywhere.

3. Huge herds developed, and ranchers needed good horsemen to herd them.

4. Barefoot Indians riding horses were called "Vaqueros" (Spanish word for cow).

5. They used a La Reata (became lariat in English). It was made from rawhide and used to rope the cows.

6. By the eighteenth century, Vaqueros had driven herds of cattle into Texas.

7. During the American Civil War, millions of longhorn cattle roamed Texas, and western United States.

8. The longhorns became wild and clustered in small herds and pawed the ground when anyone came near. The slightest noise could spook them, and they would stampede. The American cowboys had a difficult time at night during the long cattle drives.

9. The cattle, besides meat, were used for tallow for soap, candles, and hides for leather.

10. Ranchers would drive them to Kansas to the railroads to be shipped back East.

11. Places like Chicago and Kansas City were the big meat-packing places.

12. By the 1870s, most buffalo were destroyed, and longhorns had taken their place.

13. Cowboys used a variety of trails (Chisholm, Shawnee, Western, or Goodnight-loving) to get to the rail yards.

14. After the Civil War, jobs were scarce in the East, so a lot of young men discharged from military duty went to Texas to become cowboys. They would get paid one dollar to four dollars a month. There were also a lot of American Indian and Mexican cowboys as well.

15. A real cowboy was paid strictly to herd cows twenty-four hours a day.

16. He was lucky if he got to town once or twice a year.

17. He wore the same clothing and seldom carried a gun. If he did, it was worn high and snug around his waist.

18. They were not sharpshooters, but experts at roping and riding.

19. Some cowboys started at ten years old. Most were in their twenties.

20. They worked ten to fourteen hours a day plus two hours' night guard duty.

21. It was a tough, dirty, sweaty, and dangerous job. They could be kicked by a horse, killed by a charging bull, drown crossing a river, be stampeded, or quite often be hit by lightning on the open plains.

22. They were extremely loyal to their outfit and would fight to the death for it.

23. After a day's work, they would ride into camp, lay down their

saddle blankets in the rain, and sleep like dead men.

24. Next morning they would get up happy and joking around about the good times they had had in Dodge City last year.

25. Cowboys were wild and brave bunch.

26. They ate whatever the chuck wagon cook made. Sometimes they shot game along the way.

27. They wore loose fitting clothing made of cotton or flannel and a heavy woolen pants with buckskin sewed in the seat. Brown Levis became popular in the 1890s.

28. Clothes had vest pockets and heavy canvas jackets to protect them from thorns. Northern cowboys wore knee-length jackets made of sheepskin or oilskin.

29. Each cowboy had a slicker or oilskin raincoat rolled up and tied behind the saddle.

30. They wore chaps (also called shotguns) with heavy trousers. Sometimes the wider trousers had batwings. They were used for protection from mesquite or chaparral thickets.

31. Average western saddle weighed thirty pounds. It had better weight distribution than English saddle. Conchos made of German silver were round objects fastened to the saddle for decoration.

About the Author

The author was a senior mechanical designer for various defense contractors in Silicon Valley, California. He worked on aircraft, submarines, tanks, and related equipment. His watercolors have been displayed in retirement homes and art shows.

Today he is retired, and he lives in his home state with his wife, two Persian cats, and baby deer that come every day to our backyard. He has two daughters, who live nearby.

CPSIA information can be obtained
at www.ICGtesting.com
Printed in the USA
BVHW071536200223
658845BV00008B/525